E SELTSAMEN ABENTEUER DES HERRN K

S IST KALT . RABEN REDEN . IMMENSEE . REH
MAMSEL TRINKEN TEE . RABE SEHER DES
HEILS AM ABEND . ERSTE STERNE . REDE, K.
ERNSTE UNKE STARB SEHR ELEND . AM
K . NEBENAN REDET DER ESELSTRAUM . ES
LUTET DIE NASE DES ARMEN HERRN K . SEE
UNKELER SEE MER RABEN ARMEN HEISS ICH
RAEUMENDES LEBEN . RABENERDE
EBEN HEISST TRAEUMENDES . KARRENDEN NICHT
EBEN HEISST RANKENDES TRAEUMEN DEN
ELTSAMEN ABENTEUER . (DIE, ")ES HEER...

THE MAN OF JASMINE

Atlas Anti-Classics 25

UNICA ZÜRN

THE MAN OF JASMINE

& OTHER TEXTS

Translated and introduced by Malcolm Green

ATLAS PRESS   LONDON   MMXX

Published by Atlas Press, BCM Atlas Press, London WC1N 3XX.
©2020, Atlas Press.
Unica Zürn, *Der Mann im Jasmin – Eindrücke einer Geisteskrankheit*, in: Unica Zürn, *Gesamtausgabe Bd.* 4.1,
©Verlag Brinkmann & Bose, Berlin 1991, pp.135-255.
Unica Zürn, *Notizen zur letzten (?) Krise*, in: Unica Zürn, *Gesamtausgabe Bd.* 4.2,
©Verlag Brinkmann & Bose, Berlin 1998, pp.259-290;
Unica Zürn, *Das Weisse mit dem roten Punkt*, in: Unica Zürn, *Gesamtausgabe Bd.* 4.1,
©Verlag Brinkmann & Bose, Berlin 1991, pp.79-92;
Unica Zürn, *Les Jeux a deux*, in: Unica Zürn, *Gesamtausgabe Bd.* 4.1,
©Verlag Brinkmann & Bose, Berlin 1991, p. 95-110;
Unica Zürn, *Im Hinterhalt*, in: Unica Zürn, *Gesamtausgabe Bd.* 4.1,
©Verlag Brinkmann & Bose, Berlin 1991, p. 111-129.
Translation & introduction ©2020 Malcolm Green
A CIP catalogue for this book is available from the British Library.
ISBN 978-1-900565-82-0
Printed and bound by CPI, Chippenham.
UK distribution by Turnaround: www.turnaround-uk.com
USA distribution by Artbook/DAP: www.artbook.com

CONTENTS

INTRODUCTION

Malcolm Green

Unica Zürn's biography is inextricably interwoven with her work, and above all with the present book. Her texts are largely autobiographical or semi-autobiographical, and move between her fantasies, and later on her hallucinations, and the concrete events surrounding a series of serious mental crises, which in turn are catalysed by her writing. An attempt to convey her life story cannot avoid switching between these two levels almost as associatively as she herself does in *The Man of Jasmine.*

•

Born in Grunewald, Berlin, in 1916, Unica Zürn had what she later described as a "wonderful" childhood. She was deeply attached to her father, Ralph Zürn, a senior cavalry officer who was stationed in Africa and who would return to Berlin after long months of absence, looking dashing with his boots and sun tan. He would treat her as "a lady", kissing her hand, giving her exotic gifts and call her "his princess". Her love for her father is expressed vividly in her novella *Dark Spring*. By contrast, her mother, the third wife of the much older Ralph, is depicted as both egotistical and aloof, even as she as smothered the young Unica. In both *Dark Spring* and *The Man of Jasmine*, Zürn recounts a childhood (or fictional) memory of climbing into bed beside her mother and being appalled at "the mountain of tepid flesh which encloses this woman's impure spirit rolls over onto the horrified child";[1] of how the "unsatisfied woman descends on the little girl with a wet, open mouth, its naked tongue darting out, a long object like the one her brother conceals in his trousers. A deep, insurmountable aversion for her mother and for women in general was born in her."[2]

Her parents divorced in 1931 and their home, an Aladdin's cave of the fantastic objects her father had brought back from distant lands, and which often later reappeared in her hallucinations, was auctioned off. She was left with an enormous sense of loss: "In fact not a day has passed since her fifteenth year in which she has not performed these invisible walks through the house. She has never overcome the pain of having to leave this home." Zürn's description of her childhood as "wonderful" seems to be only half of the story.

On leaving school she learned shorthand and typing, and from 1933 worked as a secretary and "girl-Friday" for Ufa (Universum-Film-AG), the Germany film monopoly founded in 1919, which from its inception was intent on exploiting the propaganda value of the film industry, and she was later promoted to writing advertising copy. She remained at Ufa until 1942, seemingly unaware of the nature of the Nazi ideology that then pervaded the company. Only late in the war did she hear an illegal radio station describe the atrocities of the concentration camps, and was deeply disturbed. During her last stay in a mental hospital, some twenty-five years later, she experienced the clearest of a series of hallucinations that expressed her latent feelings of guilt: after spending the entire night awake, smoking, she realises that smoke is suffocating all the inmates of the hospital, then of Paris and the entire world, "making her a murderer as terrible as the Nazis."[3] As she noted in 1970, her hallucinations were often brought on by thoughts of the Nazi atrocities, by her shame at being a German, and by the series of harrowing abortions she later underwent out of "poverty and the inability to trust the father of the embryos."

•

A marriage in 1942 to a man much older than her produced two dearly loved children, but on divorcing him seven years later, she was left to fend for herself. The father retained custody of the children, and she received only a small sum from him, which meant she had to earn a living again. She wrote radio plays and over one hundred short stories for the newspapers; light fiction, but filled with a longing for encounters with the strange and marvellous. These productive years were not unhappy; she re-established contact with the artistic circles she had known from her time at Ufa, and painted, independently discovering the chance technique of decalcomania used by the Surrealists.

Her interest in chance encounters, and this longing for the miraculous, meant that she was already primed for the first of two encounters that were radically to change her life. The first was with Hans Bellmer. They met in 1953 through a series of accidents which read like pages from André Breton's *L'Amour Fou*: "The obsession with a particular face accompanies her for several days — see *The Man of Jasmine*.[4] Suddenly she realises that her face has a strong resemblance to the one in front of her, although this is just her imagination: the face of Hans Bellmer… She cuts off her hair in order to make her face even more like his, and practises his delicate, wistful expression in front of the mirror."[5] Bellmer was already established in Surrealist circles and the creator of a singular body of erotic drawings and sculptures, although he was wary of showing her his works, fearing she might be repelled. On the contrary, she found them intriguing.

Zürn followed Bellmer to Paris, where they lived in poverty in two small rooms in the Hotel de l'Esperance on the rue Mouffetard. Their relationship lasted almost seventeen years: "Bellmer and her, a tacit common interest, a great friendship and deep camaraderie since 1953, a great friendship… with a few shocks for her."[6] They seemed to find a deep mutual inspiration in each other. Bellmer was not only an exquisite draughtsman but also a subtle thinker, and was able to pass on his ideas to her and encouraged her to compose anagram poems. She, in turn, spurred him on to complete his major theoretical work, *The Anatomy of the Image*, and to write a text on her anagrams.[7] This text, which begins, as if in anticipation of Zürn's crises, by mentioning "the revived interest in the writings of the mentally ill, mediums and children" (all of whom she would identify with later on), describes the activity of writing anagrams as a combination of automatism, chance and an increased, feverish readiness for discovery, when "the miracle seizes us and carries us off on its broomstick."

That same year, 1953, Zürn had her first exhibition of automatic drawings in the Galerie Le Soleil dans la Tête in Paris. The opening was attended by the Surrealists, among them Breton, Man Ray, Hans Arp, Joyce Mansour and Victor Brauner, and she was accepted into their circle. Despite their enthusiasm for her work, and a series of further exhibitions in Paris and Germany, her inclusion in the large Surrealist exhibition at the Galerie Corday in 1959, and the publication of her anagram poems, Zürn's relationship with the Surrealist group seems to have been a problematic one. Years of increasing isolation followed, in which she rarely left the hotel, and then usually only in Bellmer's company. There were splits with Bellmer, followed by reconciliations, and two years when the couple stayed in Erménonville, some 50 km from Paris. Her contacts with other artists and writers arose largely through Bellmer's gallery commision for portraits: "I was allowed to accompany Bellmer during all the portrait sittings: Man Ray, Gaston Bachelard, Henri Michaux, Matta, Wilfredo Lam, Hans Arp, Victor Brauner, Max Ernst… There are those who must be adored and others who adore. I have always belonged to the latter. Being constantly full of wonder, admiration and adoration… Remaining in the background, watching and looking — that is the passive manner in which I lead my life."[8] During this period she read Hermann Melville who, she discovered, had started writing *Moby Dick* after encountering an "Irish lady" in the post coach while journeying across England. She was all too ready to believe that this encounter, which was never repeated, had precipitated Hermann Melville's greatest work.[9] Zürn longed for just such an encounter ("Three miraculous encounters that occurred in her childhood signalled to her early on that the meaning of her life would revolve around such events"), and soon afterwards she met Henri Michaux, whom she recognised as the incarnation of a man from her childhood dreams: her ideal husband. "She experiences the first 'miracle' in her life: in a room in Paris she finds herself standing before the Man of Jasmine. The shock of this encounter is so great that she is unable to recover from it. From this day on she begins, very, very slowly, to lose her reason." This encounter prompted her to write her first serious texts, including *The House of Illnesses*, *The Whiteness with the Red Spot*, and *Les Jeux à Deux* (*Games for Two*), which are all dedicated to Melville.

The years between 1957 and 1967 are documented in the text of *The Man of Jasmine* and require little comment. The cyclical nature of her crises, the contrasts between miraculous events, her feelings of megalomania, and the crushing banality and tedium of her life in mental hospitals is vividly captured. Perhaps it will suffice to note that although her first stay in the Hôpital Sainte-Anne in Paris lasted a total of three years, her "normal" spells were considerably longer. The three months in the Maison-Blanche hospital, also in Paris, described in *Notes to Her Last (?) Crisis* was her only internment during the five years between 1964 and the end of 1969. This period marked a general diminishing of her crises and an end to her attempts to break from Bellmer. It was also when her book of drawings and anagrams entitled *Oracles et Spectacles* was published, and when *The Man of Jasmine* was translated into French by her friend Ruth Henry after attempts to find a German publisher had failed. She and Bellmer had simultaneous exhibitions in Hanover in 1967, and continued to write, most importantly a lengthy text called *The Trumpets of Jericho*, a story that drew its inspiration directly from the lines of the anagrams she wove into it, and *Dark Spring*, a sombre masterpiece of forbidden childhood love and the painful awakening of sexuality, both now translated into English. However, her sanity buckled once more towards the end of 1969, when Bellmer suffered a stroke. She returned to Maison-Blanche for a month, and on leaving was confronted by the semi-paralysed Bellmer, accompanied by the psychiatrist Dr. Rabain. Bellmer feared he would be unable to cope with a recurrence of her crises and she was given the options of leaving him and returning to Germany or being admitted to a mental hospital as a preventative measure. An ambulance was already waiting outside, and because she refused the first option, she was taken away. Despite this tragic end of her relationship with Bellmer, who sent her a farewell letter promising to provide for her, this last, four-month internment was for her a "great liberation" and proved highly productive. Aged before her time, and with her life in ruins, she worked on a sequel to *The Man of Jasmine* and several other lengthy texts, some in French, while her drawings assumed an almost celebratory aspect. On her release she was unable to find anyone who would put her up (Ruth Henry was herself too ill to help), so Bellmer agreed to take her in for a few days. They spent the first evening in quiet conversation, and in the early morning she committed suicide, jumping from the sixth floor window. Bellmer placed a giant bouquet of red roses on her grave and had her headstone engraved with the words: *"Mon amour — te suivra dans l'Eternité, Hans à Unica."* Five years later he was buried beside her.

•

Various writers have offered valuable interpretations of Unica Zürn's life in light of her work,[10] showing that it is open to different readings. But rather than paraphrase their arguments (based in part on texts not included in this edition),[11] I would like to like to consider her work in the light of her partner's writings, those of Hans Bellmer.

Bellmer receives few mentions in these interpretations, which generally confine themselves to underlining his "difficult" character (and thus suggest that he was to some extent responsible for her crises), and with establishing him as one of a series of father figures in Zürn's life, along with tacitly disapproving asides.[12] Even though Zürn was sometimes critical of Bellmer, there is no overlooking the emotional support he provided, and the curious intertwining of his intellectual world with Zürn's artistic explorations and imaginings. In this way, he fitted into her life in an extraordinary manner, as if holding the key to her many mysteries. Meeting her through a series of chance events, he stepped directly into an old fantasy of hers, of meeting a doppelgänger of the other sex (the theme of a short story, "The Green Lady in the Theatre Box", written several years before), and his theoretical texts also anticipated several important themes that later appeared in her writing.

The Anatomy of the Image, begun in 1942 and completed shortly after he met Zürn, opens with a quote from Paracelsus "the scorpion heals the scorpion" (an animal that she experiences differently in her visions later on). The text contains passages that have a singular correspondence with Zürn's experiences of her splitting personality; her birth as a poet and her search for the "other", her desire to overcome her perceived limitations as a woman, and even her death. In this complex text, Bellmer argues that the transference of pain or physical stimulation from one body part to another (such as by clenching ones fist during toothache) is the underlying reflex for liberating expression: one creates a "virtual source of arousal" which, in extreme cases, can lead to the doubling of the entire individual, designated by psychiatry as the "splitting of the ego." From this simultaneous division and multiplication a new form of ego can emerge as a synthesis of the opposites thus created. As early as 1937 Bellmer had connected this virtual source of arousal with ludic forms of experimental poetry in the text *The Games of the Doll*:[13] "The best sort of game does not aim so much at a specific goal but draws its excitement from the thought of its own unforeseeable sequels — as if spurred on by an enticing promise. The best toy would therefore be one… which approaches its surroundings provocatively like a divining rod in order to discern, here and there, the feverish responses to what is always awaited and [which] everyone can repeat: The sudden images of the 'YOU'." Bellmer expands on this notion in 1954 in his essay on anagrams, in which he writes that these are born of "a violent, paradoxical conflict" between "the will to shape while simultaneously excluding all prior intention because it will prove sterile. The result appears, somewhat uncannily, to be due less to one's own consciousness than to the intervention of an 'other'."[14]

Zürn, as a medium, "the only state of which she is worthy",[15] is entranced by her anagrams and her own automatic drawings. The sense of promise, and the excitement at their predictive qualities, like those of a divining rod, to be found in the line that is to be used for an anagram poem, are clearly expressed in the pages of the present book. Words are her oracles, and the drawings look back at her from the page with the first eye that she executes. This gaze allows her to continue because she can create something that is not bound by her own contingency, which she identifies as her womanly feelings, and by what restricts her as a woman: "She finds them painful, the boundaries, limitations and monotony that are sometimes entailed simply by being a woman." More importantly, the drawing or the poem gives access to the "other" and offers her a new sense of self. Her increasing involvement with anagrams also tends, however, to cut her off from her surroundings, while filling her with a sense of courage and strength sufficient to lead a life on her own, a sensation which heralds her feelings of "megalomania". She is drawn into crises, the player becomes the "plaything", caught in the interlocking loops of word and self; she splits words into anagrams and this activity also splits her self: "splitting … the personality into an ego that *experiences* arousal and an ego that *produces* arousal." Bellmer also notes this link between the word and the bodily self: "The body resembles a sentence that seems to invite us to dismantle it into its component letters, so that its true meanings may be revealed anew through an endless stream of anagrams."[16] But an element is missing in the equation as applied to Unica Zürn's real "counterpart", for as Bellmer underlines in his essay on the image, "opposites are necessary for things to exist and for a third reality to ensue." Zürn's counterpart is still only a megalomaniac extension of herself, not the complement she longed for as a child, and which she described in *Dark Spring*.[17] She remains simply split, doubled, and can only imagine a counterpart who is visibly similar to herself, a projection of herself into a white void.

Bellmer, in his essay on the image, illustrates the phenomenon of splitting and the displacement of the source of arousal, or of elements of the self, to other parts of the body by examining a case cited by Cesare Lombroso of a fourteen-year-old "hysteric" who went blind but developed the ability to see with the tip of her nose and the lobe of her left ear, and to smell with her heels. Several years later Zürn hears "From the depths of her belly (…) the voice of a poet, whom she knows and admires, reciting an anagram that she had composed from a sentence she had found in one of his books." In a similar fashion, she displaces her own inner voices to Michaux, and believes that he is communicating telepathically with her.[18] A rash on her own skin — the starting point for her image in *The Whiteness with the Red Spot* — is likewise displaced to the "other", and becomes an external point she can clutch at in her crises: "Like someone on the verge of drowning, she seeks out a point in the room to which she can cling. This point is a small red artificial flower on top of the radio on the other side of the room. By staring at this red spot she can hold her head above the sea of torture in which she feels she is swimming. Whenever she releases her eyes from the red point, she 'drowns'."

The apparent difference between the hysteric who displaces a part of herself within her own body and Zürn, who displaces it to an outside voice, is resolved in the later chapters of Bellmer's essay, where he discusses the way in which a man and a woman can project themselves on to one another, thus "assuming the form" of the other to produce a hermaphroditic interlocking of the male and female principles through a fundamental reversibility of images and, ultimately, of the sexes.[19] Furthermore, this text suggests the missing factor in Zürn's equation: desire (her femininity, killed by her mother, or by her father, depending on whose reading one choses), when Bellmer notes that the "object or person only becomes real when desire permits it be other than it is." The self requires the other in order to be real but Zürn, the medium who awaits encounters and oracles, overhears her own desires and looks for an extension in others, while rejecting her own femininity (as she writes on numerous occasions). Her recurring fantasies about transsexuality and androgyny, and her wish to be relieved of the mystery of the sexes ("How good I would feel if I could be something that called itself neither man nor woman")[20] do not take her so far as the daring hermaphroditism proposed by Bellmer. For Zürn the reversibility of the sexes and of images, remains unidirectional. She waits passively, responds to signs in her surroundings (the ever-recurring "HM" — Hermann Melville, Henri Michaux, the initials of the Hôtel Minerve on a towel, her chance meetings with Bellmer even), but still the "reversibility" of the image, of the alter ego with self, lacks the "third reality". She is unable to make of it something resembling the "objective chance" advocated by Breton, it remains simply hallucination and delusion.

Unable to take part in the defining of situations by means of desire, because she lacks a real counterpart with whom to interact, and addicted to the shimmering "other" she found in her anagrams, a part from her own ego splits off ("the kobold behind the ego" — Bellmer), so that she remains merely a *virtual* existence: "After forty-three years this life has not become "*my* life" (my italics). It might just as well be someone else's life."[21] Even her suicide seems to have been dictated from outside, to have been overdetermined: her father's first wife, a writer with whom Zürn identified, killed herself by jumping out of the window of a psychiatric hospital, in common with her Uncle Falada, with whom she likewise identifies in a passage in *The Man of Jasmine*. The only suicides or suicide attempts mentioned in *The Man of Jasmine* are by defenestration. Indeed, Bellmer described precisely such a death as an example of an aspect of the reversibility of the image in *The Doll*. Zürn, for her own part, had described this method of suicide in *Dark Spring* three years earlier. As Inge Morgenroth points out, the link between her means of death and the window has a deeper significance. In *Dark Spring*, Zürn wrote: "When she lies in her room in order to sleep, she studies the cross formed by the window panes. The vertical line is the man, the horizontal the woman. The point where the two lines meet is a mystery." Later, she looks at the cross after masturbating on her bed and longs for a male complement. At the tragic end of the story, the girl's plunge to her death from the window concludes with the family dog approaching her and licking her genitals, repeating the one happy, innocent sexual encounter she had experienced.

•

Zürn's texts suck us deep into her world; it is as difficult to free oneself as it was for the writer herself. In spite, or perhaps because of, her use of the third person (Zürn's original manuscript of *The Man of Jasmine* even attributed the book to "the wife of Hans Bellmer"). Her agency is thus removed, like that of the central character, almost as if she has become a medium to her own self. Occasionally she rebels, however. *The Whiteness with the Red Spot*, written in the first person, is an angry condemnation of her contingency, her "training", of the illusions of hope and happiness she had projected onto the other, the "white man". Two shorter texts, *The House of Illnesses* (see the final page of this book for information on the Atlas Press edition) and *Les Jeux à Deux* (*Games for Two*) employ a laconic humour to similar effect. Her anagrams also reveal an overt aggression; the German words for "*The Whiteness with the Red Spot*" became transformed into: "the chamber of wounds, plague-raging-murder. If it stinks to you, spit it out." In the lines of the anagram poems she incorporates into *In Ambush* we read, among others:

"Thunderously igniting lusts with hissing church-oil thunder." And if the main texts seem strangely subdued and obedient by comparison, it should not be forgotten that they were written under a strong inner compulsion, against the advice of others (her assertion that Dr. Rabain encouraged her to write *The Man of Jasmine* was strongly denied by him), that it jeopardised her "normal" state. The importance she attached to the work is evident from the efforts she took to have it published. Her use of the third person voice allowed her to she neutralise her subjectivity, which, far from being an expression of "passivity," conveys the violence and destitution she experienced in mental institutions with disarming objectivity. Even if the formal quality of her syntax sometimes seems like a mechanism of self-preservation, a means of maintaining control or of avoiding direct answers to the question "why?", it should be noted that the only other possibility, writing in the first person, would be no less limiting. In one of the few comparable works available to us, Gerard de Nerval's *Aurelia*, although the author writes in the first person, he frequently resorts to the passive tense in order to convey his madness; Nerval, we would do well to remember, was an established writer who was not in danger of sounding like an "irrational *woman*," which was the initial reception accorded *The Man of Jasmine* in Germany.

Zürn is the medium of her experiences in an active sense; an apparent coolness frees her from the hackneyed language of the self, grants coincidences, encounters and miracles what she considers to be their correct weight and value, and allows her to document her experiences without censorship or judgement. In the end we are forced to the conclusion that Zürn's acumen and artistry, and her virtuosity as a writer, were able to withstand her mental crises and depressions, allowing her to add a further masterpiece to that small, precious row of unclassifiable works that includes Breton's *Nadja*, Nerval's *Aurelia* and Leonora Carrington's *Down Below*.

NOTE TO THIS EDITION

The Man of Jasmine was first published by Gallimard in 1971 in Ruth Henry's translation under the title *L'Homme-Jasmin*, followed by the German edition in 1975. Both contained the same selection of texts: *The Man of Jasmine, Impressions from a Mental Illness* (1965-1967); *Notes from her Last (?) Crisis* (1967); *The Whiteness with the Red Spot* (1959); *Les Jeux à Deux* (1959); *The House of Illnesses* (1958); the French edition had a foreword by André Pierre de Mandiargues, the German appeared with brief texts by Ruth Henry and Dr. Jean-Francois Rabain. The present edition differs in two respects: *The Whiteness with the Red Spot* has been translated from the original, un-amended text, and the last piece has been replaced with *In Ambush* (1963) in order to allow *The House of Illnesses* to be published separately in a facsimile edition with the all-important drawings referring to the text. This new English edition has been revised using the definitive edition of Zürn's *Gesamtausgabe* (*Complete Works*) published by Brinkmann und Böse Verlag, Berlin, 1998-2001.

The anagrams pose an obvious problem of translation. Literal versions have been given, with the German original as footnotes.

THE MAN OF JASMINE

IMPRESSIONS FROM A MENTAL ILLNESS

One night in the sixth year of her life a dream conducts her behind the tall mirror which hangs in a mahogany frame on the wall of her room. This mirror becomes an open door through which she steps to reach a long avenue lined with poplars that leads in a straight line to a small house. The front door of the house is open. She enters and finds herself before a staircase, which she climbs. She does not encounter anyone. She stops in front of a table. On the table is a small white card. As she picks up the card to read the name on it, she awakens. The impression of this dream is so strong that she gets up in order to push the mirror to one side. There is only the wall and no door.

That morning, filled with an inexplicable loneliness, she enters her mother's room in order to get into her bed and return, if possible, to whence she came and to see nothing any more.

The mountain of tepid flesh that encloses this woman's impure spirit rolls over onto the horrified child, who flees forever from the mother, the woman, the spider! She is deeply mortified.

Then the vision appears to her for the first time: The Man of Jasmine! Boundless consolation! Sighing with relief, she sits down opposite him and studies him. He is paralysed! What luck! He will never leave his seat in the garden where the jasmine blossoms even in winter.

This man becomes for her the image of love. *These* eyes are blue in a way which is more beautiful than any eyes she has ever seen.

So she marries him. The loveliest thing is that no one knows. This is her first, her greatest secret.

His silent presence teaches her two lessons which she never forgets:

Distance.

Passivity.

Much later on, one key after another is turned inside her, but she does not open herself up. Quickly tiring of her, people cast this casket aside as useless, especially because during the years that follow, whenever she looks over a male shoulder she is leaning on, she sees The Man of Jasmine behind. She remains faithful to her childhood marriage.

1957, in the village of Ermenonville, not far from Paris, she writes six short manuscripts in an attempt to free herself from an impression that has become too powerful. But she does not succeed: "What happiness to be at that point before the start of everything. Nothing can be done to us because we are unable to do anything unto ourselves."

As a million red blood corpuscles desert her, as her body is covered by the countless red spots of an allergy, she writes in her *Notes of an Anaemic*: "Someone is travelling inside me, crossing from one side to the other. I have become his home. Outside, in the black landscape with the bellowing cow, someone is maintaining that they exist. The circle spelt out by his gaze closes around me. Traversed by him within, encircled by him from without — this is my new situation. And I like it."

During the night she dreams of a beautiful, dangerous creature: a girl and a snake in one — with long tresses. It plots to destroy all that surrounds it. A careful operation must be performed upon it so as to remove anything it might use to wreak this destruction. Its brain is removed, its heart, its blood and its tongue. Most essentially, its eyes are removed, but they forget to remove its hair. That was their one mistake, for the creature — blind, bloodless and dumb — now attains such enormous power that there is no alternative but for all who surround it to flee for their lives. What does this signify?

A few days later she experiences the first miracle in her life: in a room in Paris she finds herself standing before the Man of Jasmine. The shock of this encounter is so great that she is unable to recover from it.

From this day on she begins, very, very slowly, to lose her reason.

This man's appearance is identical to the image from her childhood vision. The only difference is that he is not paralysed, nor surrounded by a garden of blossoming jasmine.

She suddenly becomes engrossed in a manuscript "in honour of the number 9" as a way of shutting herself off in her thoughts and thus of forgetting reality.

This number assumes the greatest significance for her. She writes: "If you say the 9-times table out loud, you descend a ladder — like a music scale, because:

Once 9 is nine

2 times 9 is eighteen

3 times 9 is twenty-seven

4 times 9 is thirty-six

5 times 9 is forty-five

6 times 9 is fifty-four

7 times 9 is sixty-three

8 times 9 is seventy-two

9 times 9 is eighty-one…

This reveals to her the sheer beauty of mathematics for the first time.

Yet that is not the end of it.

The things she had learned as a school-child tempt her to keep arriving at the number 9 by other means as well. She adds up the digits in 18, 27, 36, 45, 54, 63, 72, 81 and ends up with 9. For:

1 plus 8 is 9

2 plus 7 is 9

3 plus 6 is 9

4 plus 5 is 9 — etc.

"What does the man born in the year 99 say when he wakes on the first day of the year 66? Over the course of time his lovely 99 has gone and stood on its head, and there's no need to tell him what that means. The 66 is about to plunge with him head over heels into eternity."

Her curiosity about the form of other numbers is now awakened. She studies the number 8. She cuts it vertically down the middle and ends up with a pair of threes which look at each other eye to eye.

Her zodiac sign — Cancer — is represented by a slightly slanting, floating 69, and to her European eye the famous Chinese symbol for Tai-Gi (primal beginning) looks like 69.

She thinks of the figure 9 as a person standing upright, his gaze turned to the left — the direction from which, to her mind, the unexpected always seems to come, although she can't say why. When a 9 meets a 9 she allows them to turn face to face until, filled with emotion, they let their foreheads touch while down below their feet have already started to fuse.

Now they form the shape of a heart.

Likewise she lets two sixes turn face to face and sees the ace of spades.

She draws the 9 once more, continuing its gentle curve downwards and attaching the loop of the 6 at the bottom: the figure 8 appears — infinity standing upright. It reminds her of an hourglass.

She makes 9 the number of life, 6 the number of death, and both numbers are hidden within the figure 8.

During this period she starts to draw snakes and is deeply moved by this animal's abilities because it can form, if it wants, a 9, a 6, an 8 and a 3, and above all a perfect circle with its own body.

Her preoccupation with 9 and 6 becomes a mania. Suddenly she starts to encounter these numbers on every corner.

She is very happy when, during this time of preoccupation, she receives a beautiful 999 from the ticket machine at a Paris bus-stop.

She attends a large protest meeting against the atom bomb and contracts jaundice. Feverish and lying in bed, she produces the manuscript of *The House of Illnesses*.

"Wishes are forbidden," Mortimer, the doctor, says to her in this house. "Wishing is detrimental to your health. I forbid you to do it. These stories about people being granted their last wishes are old wives' tales. You are very sick, because someone has shot out the two hearts in your eyes. It's no wonder that you now must keep looking to the left — it is in that direction that your murderer lurks."

Ah, he struck me as incredibly stupid, this Mortimer, but before leaving this house I secretly opened the door to the "Room of Eyes".

Suddenly the red scorpion leapt from the ceiling and with an appalling gesture pierced its heart with its own sting. At the same moment the white eagle flew in through the open window and embraced me in its wonderful blue eyes.

Then, far away from here, it put its wings away and returned to its room. It sits opposite the empty armchair and watches the passing of time with perplexity.

She writes her manuscript titled *Les Jeux à Deux*.

It includes The Game of Extension (because the first time she saw him in his room he had been an incredible three metres tall); The Game of Incorporation (because she *feels* that he is incorporating her into himself in order once again to destroy her inside himself, and thus make their encounter null and void); The Game of Harmony (because he lies down, outstretched, within her body as she falls asleep, and they rest in one another as if in a sarcophagus. He slips away the moment she opens her eyes the next morning).

Another night she meets him on a sunny plateau and they set out on a wordless walk together. How delightful: he is not paralysed! And he has the same beautiful detachment as the Man of Jasmine. Ceaseless amazement at the fact that a vision has become reality!

The following night, when she wants to dream with him, she finds herself outside his closed door.

It's over!

Due to her lack of intelligence, she wants desperately to believe that he is "hypnotising" her. Her brain, small as a chicken's, is unable grasp that it is *she* who has hypnotised herself by allowing her thoughts to revolve time and again about the same person. He is the eagle describing circles above the masochistic chicken. She has been presented with this situation. There is no way out. She starts to get confused. The first crisis begins in a cinema. She sees him enter just as the lights dim. He takes a seat several rows away, right behind her.

An ad begins for a certain type of oil. Bottles filled with oil appear one after another until she finds the sight of them unbearable. The bottles turn into a symbol of the male member — this gives her such a feeling of nausea that she fears she must vomit.

The second film follows: someone is being rescued following an accident in the mountains. The young man is pulled up from a crevasse on a rope. In her mind the image is telling her that her son is in mortal danger.

This is followed by the English film *The League of Gentlemen*.[22]

Five gentleman gangsters rob a bank. She gets the impression from the film that *she herself* is the bank, which is not being robbed but abducted, as if being led to a new destiny. It reminds her of a game from her childhood: "Robbers and Princesses."

For her the five gentlemen gangsters become a kind of secret "fifth column" that will appear whenever she is in danger — saviours in her hour of need. An "unknown" organisation.

Why has she moved to France?

In 1953, in Berlin, she watched the same French film three times in order to get drunk on the sight of a particular face that hasn't the slightest similarity to that of the Man of Jasmine.

She identifies so strongly with this masculine face that she is suddenly told, "you resemble him."

A few days later she meets a man and recognises him as the one in the film, whose face her own has come to resemble. Greatly surprised, she hears someone say: "That man looks like X, the film star."

This confirmation, as well as his invitation to her to accompany him to Paris, spurs her decision to leave Berlin. This friend[23] talks to her about anagrams and shows her how to make poems from them. At the same time he discovers her talent for automatic drawings and encourages her, a year later he is able to arrange for her first book, *Hexentexte* to be published by Galerie Spranger in Berlin. In Paris she meets the "Man of Jasmine".

That evening, after seeing *The League of Gentlemen*, she finds two red initials on her towel: HM (the monogram of the hotel in which she is staying: the Hôtel Minerve). It is the monogram of the man to whom, for a specific reason, she has dedicated the six short manuscripts she wrote in Ermenonville: Herman Melville.

She had read that he started writing *Moby Dick* after meeting an "Irish lady in the mail-coach while journeying across England."

She was all too ready to believe that this meeting, which was never repeated, had precipitated Herman Melville's greatest work. She had composed her own short manuscripts — of no value — under the spell of a meeting, and, slightly dramatically, had sent them to the Man of Jasmine, asking him to burn them.

Three miraculous encounters that occurred in her childhood signalled to her early on that the meaning of her life would revolve around such events.

After the vision of the Man of Jasmine she is taken to meet a very aged Sioux chieftain, Big Chief White Horse Eagle. He presses a kiss on her hand and the hand turns black. She refuses to wash the kiss away.

A few days later she meets the pygmy, no taller than herself. He places his small black hands beneath his left cheek. He closes his eyes, bows his head and starts slowly to rock: the gesture of sleeping.

Three steps further and she stops before a Hindu who presents her with a hot ball of rice, rolled together with curry, on the palm of his hand. Now she has four strange kings: the white, the red, the black and the brown!

So when the red HM — the monogram of the "white man" — stares up at her in this alien hotel room it can only mean one thing: an encounter!

She switches off the light, opens the window and goes to bed. A group of men rush up the stairs. The door of the room across the corridor opens, someone enters. The room remains in darkness. The fifth column?

She waits. She *knows* — something will happen now. There! The first sign from ACROSS THE WAY! A clear, sharp ring. A note. As if someone were striking a triangle: "PING!" Whether she wishes it or not, this "PING" is a command. She sits up. What next? The signal sounds several times, and, as if drawn by a silver thread, she leaves the room "in order to prepare herself for an operation." What a strange ceremony! "They" ask her to empty herself, if possible, of the residue of all the years, like a surgeon requesting one to evacuate before making the first incision. She feels so thin — like a leaf of white paper. But the PING! PING! PING! rings out again, and on returning she has become transparent. She is like white nothingness.

PING!

She lies down. Waiting. The Hindus who she has just met carrying a sleeping child in the corridor appear for a moment in the lit-up window of another room across the way. A curtain is drawn and through it appears a soft, round light which slowly begins to rotate like the beam of a lighthouse. A wonderful, calming motion.

PING!

Suddenly a curious white airfield appears, like a giant photograph in the night sky outside her open window. But no! The scene is in motion. It's like a film projected on the sky. People are crossing the airfield and boarding the plane. Suddenly she sees *him* in the foreground, just as she had seen him the first time as a child — but standing erect and she in his arms, aged six, "on the day she married him."

Completely astonished, she observes the two of them boarding the plane, then watches as it ascends and disappears into the sky.

The sky is black once more, there is nothing to be seen. PING! PING! PING! PING!

She waits.

A picture of terrible solitude is revealed: a cellar with empty bottles — and all in white. Among the bottles is her son's head, inclined to one side. A white marble head with white curls that enfold it in baroque patterns. He has hanged himself. She summons all her will-power so as to help her dying son to a speedy death. She remains strangely dispassionate at the sight of this image. Her sole concern is that he should not suffer. And at last his head droops, his eyes close — it's over. She recalls the scene in the film she had seen that day: the rope above the head of the injured man in the mountains. That was the preparation for the image she sees *now*.

She is unaware that she is having hallucinations. In her present state, the most incredible things, hitherto unseen, become reality, so that when these images appear to her in the night sky, they are *really* there.

As the PING-PING-PING-PING resounds once more from across the way, she knows that it is *he* who is making this noise, and, momentarily at a loss, she thinks that it is hypnotism. That would be a reasonable explanation.

The sky remains dark. All she can see are the black silhouettes of four chimneys. She stares at these vertical forms for a long time without grasping their meaning, until a single PING rings out with great force — and then she is *certain* that the four shapes are four graves. *His* graves! Four dead people whom he loves? She knows nothing about him. The image of these graves is intended — she realises — to mark a *boundary* that must not to be crossed. Suddenly the sound of a man weeping in despair comes from outside her door: unrestrained sobs like she has never heard before. He is mourning his dead. Yet when she leaves her room in order, if at all possible, to console him, there is no one there. He has returned to the dark room opposite hers. She lies down and remains awake.

Now feeling very unhappy, she hesitantly relates to him her story, which is no less sad than his.

As morning appears, she places six white paper handkerchiefs in a metal container and sets them alight. White smoke rises vertically to the ceiling, and in the smoke she sees his tall and growing figure, and his face, which becomes clearly recognisable.

Later, over breakfast, she reads an item in the *Le Monde*:

"The young Abbé Christian … was discovered hanging in the forest of ——." She writes a letter to the boarding school in Germany where her son is staying, as if this man was her own son whose death she had actually *seen* that night. The letter contains an anagram which she has devised from the sentence *Ye would have plucked out your own eyes* (*Ihr haettet Eure Augen ausgerissen*), which she had found in Galatians 4, 15: "Where is then the blessedness ye spake of? For I bear you record, that, if it had been possible, ye would have plucked out your own eyes, and have given them to me."

The anagram poem reads:

The dictum of your day: hard
Of your eyes: being.
Your skin is song — your advice: understand.
Your house is masked. Your victories close.
Your deed: a resting place united with a coffin.[24]

She posts this letter, which resembles an epitaph. It is the first crazy message she will send.

(Anagrams are words and sentences created by rearranging the letters from a different word or sentence. One may only use the letters that are available, and not draw on any others. Inventing anagrams is one of her most intense preoccupations.)

Later she learns that the boarding-school has notified the father about the letter, who, appalled, sets off there at once, only to discover of course that his son is still alive.

In another anagram written during her involvement with the number 9 she takes the phrase:

Our number of destiny in ninety-nine (Unsere Schicksalszahl ist die neunundneunzig).

She finds this anagram:

Now his contemplative eye seeks you as its target. Short
are our days and they sink all too fast to ice. — Oh! [25]

Or she poses the question:

Shall I meet you some day? (Werde ich Dir einmal begegnen?)

The anagram of this sentence gives her the following answer:

After three paths in the rain, form
your counter-image on waking: He —
the magician! — Angels weave you into
the dragon's body. — Rings in the way —
I shall be yours for long, in the rain.[26]

Looking at one sentence and searching for another is an inexhaustible source of pleasure for her. The concentration and enormous quiet this work requires allow her to shut herself off completely from her surroundings — indeed to forget reality, which is what she wants.

On one occasion she took the sentence: *Behind this unblemished brow (Hinter dieser reinen Stirne)* and found within it these anagrams:

Behind this unblemished brow
a man speaks, a sense travels,
a star strays into his herd,
a silky steer runs. Here
the rider Hindsense, his
nests beyond India — Mad-lake
Madness, cheerfulness. Duck
of the three ink-men — if they travel
— an obstacle! — Saviour of his
ink-men — is it a madwoman?[27]

The last question in her anagram, "is it a madwoman?" had captivated her during that time in Ermenonville, because obviously it related to herself.

When seeking and finding anagrams, and when executing the first, the very first stroke on the white paper after dipping her pen in black Chinese ink, not knowing just *what* she will draw, it is then that she feels the excitement and the great curiosity that is needed if one is to be surprised by one's own work.

Lost to all rational reasoning or considerations, she breaks off the long, serious friendship with the man who had brought her to Paris so as to share his life with her. She makes up her mind to return to Berlin and begin a new life. She feels strong and courageous. Able to do anything!

She spends these last days in Paris staying with friends, and asks them to play her some wonderful, powerful music. She asks to hear Beethoven's *Ode to Joy*, but this choral, which at other times had thrilled and moved her, now sounds weak and banal to her. Perhaps on this day she would have preferred the famous Trumpets of Jericho — music that heralds a great fall.

Lost in thought, she remains stretched out on a bed, when suddenly the inside of her body gives clear replies to the questions she asks herself.

This impression is so astonishing that she asks her friends whether a microphone has been built into the bed and is producing these high or low sounds which almost resemble short words.

In the night these vague sounds inside her body become a comprehensible language. From the depths of her belly she hears the voice of a poet, whom she knows and admires, reciting an anagram that she had composed from a sentence she had found in one of his books. This sentence runs: *And shave off your little rosy beard (Und scheert ihr Rosenbaertlein ab).*[28]

He recites this anagram in a deep and infinitely soothing voice:

Tristan beside Isolde. Acrid smoke
strays over this hard life. The larks
build their nest in the already pale
pear of star-red hand. But it is snowing
red — grape-red valerian-peace.[29]

And suddenly — as if in greeting — this poet's long, highly distinctive nose appears on her pillow. It is like one of those incredible noses she had admired in a book of Japanese ghost stories.

The room is quiet and dark — she waits — she *knows* — that there is more to come. Her state of mind is quite out of the ordinary — everything is possible!

There! A small, delightful sewing machine is floating in the air a metre above her head. It is an old-fashioned model, like those she remembers from her childhood — but this sewing machine is *coloured*: black–gold and red. A lot of red in fact! The tiny wheels turn silently, the needle pecks up and down like a bird's beak. The reel spins round with its white yarn. The machine is sewing, but no human hand, nor foot, can be seen setting it in motion.

And *now* she understands this image. She recalls a sentence from a poem she had read long ago and never forgotten, for the sentence conveys an atmosphere that seems to come from another world: "Someone is sewing! Is it you?"

That morning she had sent the white man a folder of her drawings. On the last page she had stuck a red star she had bound about with white sewing thread.

She had written this particular sentence around the star in French. And *he* sends *her* this really charming hallucination by way of an answer and a gift.

Merci!

The manifestation disappears — much to her regret — and something completely new appears. Something which she had never pictured before in her imagination.

Large shapes — like wings — float up to her, opening and closing — gently at first — until they slowly fill the room and she has the impression that she is in the presence of apparitions that have no relationship to this world. Not a single one of her acquaintances has ever mentioned apparitions like these to her. These beings — she cannot describe them any other way — reveal the clear and frightening intention of encircling her. They exude a sense of dissipation, of annihilation, and her forgotten childhood fear of the horrible and inexplicable returns to her. Whenever these birdless, greyish-black wings fly up too close to her she raises her hand in sudden alarm and fends them off. They retreat for a moment into the background of the dark room, then approach once again, and slowly she gets used to their strange presence until she notices that the wings are insubstantial and can fly straight through her upright body, as if she had become bodiless. This both entrances and appals her. Looking at them carefully, these creatures have in fact nothing terrifying about them — they lack eyes and faces, and they radiate great dignity, an incredible seriousness and something very noble.

She would happily go mad if she were told her that it was necessary to go mad in order to experience such hallucinations, especially this last one. It remains the most astonishing thing she has ever seen.

Once these apparitions have gradually faded, she turns on the light in order to investigate the room: she is convinced that she will be able to find him somewhere. The experience of seeing something appear out of nothing is so inordinate that she can think of no other explanation than direct hypnosis. Her friends come and convince her that there is no "hypnotist" in the apartment. They stay with her until morning. As dawn breaks she opens the window and sees the dustmen at work on the street far below. From this great distance she recognises clearly one of her friends from Berlin, the actor Ernst Schröder, and calls out his name: ERNST!

This word sounds appalling to her in the quiet of the street — as if it meant: "Things are starting to get earnest."[30]

Suddenly aware that shortly she must leave this city she loves, she throws a glass at the wall, and her friends look at her in alarm. She is taken to Orly Airport by taxi. With a second desperate gesture she throws her red spectacle case out of the car — like the children in the fairy tale who cast bread behind them in order to leave a trail with which to find their way back out of the maze of the forest into which they are being lead.

While waiting in the hall at Orly for her plane to Frankfurt, she cuts a 6 on the palm of her left hand with the sharp tip of a nail-file. For suddenly her lovely number of life — the number 9 — has become for her the 6. And while performing this painful operation, she thinks of the anagram she had made from the sentence:

When nine has become six (*Wenn die Neun zur Sechs geworden ist*).

The result:

Where does it rain between nine and three? It
rains so new between us. The nine of the
winds has turned into six. When the
paths are red, run yourself white to us. We
shall die in order to triumph! Hours, lovely
for blushing. In silence, now knowing.[31]

The six is marked in blood on her hand. She had felt no pain. She walks out onto the street for a moment without knowing why. A large black car drives up — she raises her arms — (she *has* to do it) — with an imploring gesture and jumps into the car — because:

This black car has assumed for her the meaning of the coming war, and she wishes to hinder this war with her gesture. And she does stop this "war": the car halts. The driver gives her a startled look.

After this scene there is a blank in her memory, for she cannot remember just how she had arrived inside the plane. As she boards she hears the voice of a man she recognises: "She doesn't see a soul!" So, there are people aboard who are acquainted her! And indeed she had received a curious "order" from him: "Lower your eyes — don't look at anyone!"

She hears the voices of other travellers on the plane whom she knows: the doctor from Essen; the art dealer from Berlin. So "witnesses" are present: "something has to be verified." They are performing an experiment on her! She has to pass certain tests! So everything must be on the level. Slowly she gains the impression that she is a medium. She asks the steward for a pack of cigarettes and suddenly recognises him as a young bookseller from Paris (Flinker). So they have sent her a "knight" to accompany her on her journey. She reads the following words on the cigarette packet: *"Félicitations de l'Air France!"*

She *reads* these words! So they really are printed on the packet.

She is being congratulated!

Something has been planned for her during the flight. She is astonished when she grasps this: *who* could have thought it all up? The idea is that when a totally black aeroplane appears, with a small white circle on its left wing, she must get to it by taking a daring leap through the air and then fly off to her *real* life, which she has yet to discover but has sometimes sensed. She will accomplish this incredible aerialist feat with the greatest of ease, because for several days now she has had the impression that she can do anything she wants or that is suggested to her. She gets up and walks to the door so as not to miss the black aeroplane. But the bookseller from Paris is friendly enough to take her back to her seat and tell her that it is not yet time to disembark.

On reaching Frankfurt he asks her whether she had done the drawings in the portfolio which he had just been admiring. She says yes, and he gives her a wave as she disembarks. But in this moment she sees the black aeroplane with the small white circle on its left wing climb and slowly disappear. With tears in her eyes she raises her hand and waves after it… Why, oh why hadn't it waited for her?

Inside the terminal at Frankfurt Airport, where she must wait for the plane to Berlin, she sits down on her own beside a large white vase. It is so beautiful she doesn't dare place her white paper handkerchief inside and light it with a match — so that she will see the white man, who she can no longer call the Man of Jasmine, appear in the rising cloud of smoke.

But he raises his voice once again inside her and repeats his command: "Don't look at anyone. Lower your eyes to your feet — and walk."

That's all. She stands up, and several steps ahead of her, she sees a large, black iron coat-stand that looks threatening. And she gets the impression that this is a prison. "Step inside!"

She winds her way with a difficult and painful movement between the black bars until she is inside. She feels ashamed and humiliated.

Being commanded not to look at anyone perhaps spares her from seeing the people who form a circle round her and stare. Then an "ambassador" — an "initiate" — appears in the form of a French steward who invites her to continue her journey to Berlin: the plane is waiting. In order to be quite certain that he knows *everything* he should in this situation, she asks him to name a letter of the alphabet and a number. Without hesitation he answers: "L–H–M–6–9"

So she twists her way back out of her prison and, perfectly trusting, allows herself to be taken to the aeroplane.

Her friends are waiting for her at Tempelhof Airport in Berlin. Dressed from head to toe in black and carrying the large box filled with her drawings under her arm, she goes over to meet them. Later they tell her: "That looked really crazy, the way you walked over to us across the airfield." And this is the first time this word is spoken in front of her. She takes it quite for granted — she likes this word: crazy.

It is an emotional shock for her to see her city again after being away for so long. As if she only *now* senses how much she loves the city of her childhood. She knows: the city is divided in two. An unsettling state for a city. So, secretly she resolves to make this city arise anew, in perfect unity. And it is *she* who will give birth to this city. This wish becomes so enormous that she has labour pains — the same sensations as during the birth of her children. She does not know how it is possible to feel pregnant with an entire city. But she has been experiencing incredible things for several days, so that this *new* state seems almost natural to her.

From that moment on she meets small groups of children on every street she walks along — small "fifth columns" — and she sees that this is a sign that she is expected. The dustbins are being emptied in all the courtyards she passes, and the autumn leaves are swept away from in front of her feet. Is the city already preparing itself for its new birth?

Whenever she enters a shop to purchase something, she leaves behind far more money than it costs, and departs the shop with the words: "Happy birthday and many happy returns." Naturally, the people in the shops are enchanted. She encounters one large smile wherever she goes. She also starts to walk in a completely new way: very fast and incredibly nimble. It seems to her as if she were floating two centimetres above the pavement — she's flying!

She is certain that soon a large party will be thrown. She dashes off hasty messages on white paper, addresses them to the poets she loves, rolls them up and lets these white birds of her apotheosis fly out of the window.

A tall Negro — a musician — appears at her friends' home. He accompanies her to a stationer's where she wants to buy something. Before they enter he folds his hands and turns his eyes to heaven. On returning, she tells her friends: "He prayed for me."

And her friends say to her: "Other people saw it as well." So it is true.

When no one is at home in the apartment she hears her friends' voices from the windows across the way, sounding so joyful, as if the party was being organised without her being allowed to see the preparations — as if they wanted to surprise her. She no longer undresses when she goes to bed at night. There is a very tall ladder leaning against the wall right outside her window. What can that mean? Will someone take this romantic route to appear by night, to rob her, take her to the place where, after so much time spent waiting, she will finally begin the life that is actually destined for her? For she cannot come to terms with the thought that what she has experienced till now was simply it. That would be far too paltry.

Like the princess in Andersen's fairy tale she plays "A guest is coming" (that game of inordinate solitude) all on her own. She remains awake the whole night long. She requires no food.

She is filled with great joy and anticipation. As if to invoke his appearance — (three metres tall!) — she reads once again the anagrams she has composed from the sentence: *The genie from the bottle* (*Der Geist aus der Flasche*), taken from the tale in *The Thousand and One Nights*. It was the most fertile sentence she had ever found and mined for anagrams, and resulted in 9 different anagrams which she came up with in Palavas-les-Flots. A few of them should be given:

Climb out of the bottle! He shall
win who climbs out the bottle
as the quill greets. Oh —
sea-eagle, freshness, you, my day!

The genie from the bottle
questions you. He who might read it,
the ghastly noble, grasped
you hideously. Rock of branches,
say that it roars. The fields,
as the fire stirred,
lay earth, freshness of the dew.

Thirst as plumage, ashes
of glass, fished the earth's
poison. Rustle, speak from the
barrel's good liquor, which
the witch's corpse devoured, said
the genie from the bottle.

Say it from the quill's light,
flow, day of horror,
read the face of the woman.
May the dew climb out of the
bottle. The river's noble
grass-freshness, oh, days numbering three.

The plumage rustles,
sleep is no more. May the bottle's
talking climb out of the
figure. Speak as soft as the
genie's smoke, for the rock of
the eye refreshes nobility.

I greet old things: quill,
butterfly, sheath of grey.

Tell the woman: light of the
devil, so that the wicked one —
the genie from the bottle —
will laugh from his gob.[32]

That night his laughter rings out from a brightly lit window opposite hers —
as heart-rending as the weeping outside her door in the Paris hotel. This is how
he announces his presence to her. She gets up and looks at the window in the house
opposite. She sees him sitting at his desk in the calm light of a reading lamp. He
is writing. She turns on the radio and hears the English bank robber from *The
League of Gentlemen* give a short speech, with a sly laugh. Naturally it is addressed
to her. Ah! She understands. The speech comes from his room opposite hers. What
a delightful idea of his! Then she hears on this radio — which is linked to him —
the wonderful light-footed and light-hearted music from the days when she was a
young girl: waltzes — waltzes — the loveliest dance for two in the Western world!

This man is charming to her. How well he has thought out this programme for
her! What skilful staging!

What words he said to her as she bade him farewell: *"On peut s'amuser tout
seul!"*[33]

Ah! People are on their way over to see her!

Hadn't she seen her brother that morning? He went missing at Vitebsk during
the last war, but she had never believed him dead.

This morning he had entered her flat, as if knowing that she was here, and
shaken her firmly by the hand.

She had not made any mention of this visit to her friends, so as to keep his
secret from others. Only the little girl who had been with her at the time and had
opened the door to the "stranger" is in the know. When her parents later ask her
whether anyone had called, the child replies. "No."

That is mysterious.

Was she the only one who saw him? Had he made himself invisible to the
child's eyes?

That night, after the lovely music has faded, she expects a visit from four men and prepares gifts for them which she arranges on the chairs. She decides that Christmas has arrived. It is autumn, but for her it is Christmas. She expects her brother. She also expects her father, who had confided in his last conversation with her, before going to Rapallo, that he would like to enter a monastery. Although she had received certain news of his death, she has never given up hope of seeing him again. So he will come. The third person will be her son. The fourth, the white man.

Now she suddenly understands the secret of her son's astonishing blue eyes. She recalls the winter evening when a strange, empty moment descended on her: she was standing in front of her husband's writing desk when she fell into a state of complete abstraction. She was alone in the flat. The last thing she can remember of that evening is the sight of the writing desk. The next day she awoke in her bed. During that night, in which she had not felt her husband's touch, the white man had given life to her son, and nine months later he was born with *his* blue eyes. That deep peace — the indescribable harmony she experienced as long as this child rested inside her body, turns into a never-ending scream the moment he releases himself from her forever.

She is given ether during her labour; she feels no pain but hears herself screaming, as if already screaming at the horrors of her coming fate which was sealed by her separation from her son.

She spends the night recollecting her childhood memories with a wonderful clarity.

Once again she repeats her countless mental walks round the house and garden of her childhood in Grunewald. She walks up and down the stairs, through all twelve rooms, and gazes into the winter fire in the hearth of the large hall. She touches the Asian and Arabian furniture her father had brought back from his travels, and which, rather than making a museum of the house, had turned it into a beautiful cave that stirred the imagination.

She looks at each object, every picture, at all of the shapes and colours.

This is a memory exercise she has repeated to the point of perfection over the years that followed the great auction in which everything, almost everything she had grown up with, was sold off. In fact, not a day has passed since her fifteenth year on which she has not performed these invisible walks through the house. She has never overcome the pain of having to leave this home.

And tonight, convinced by his thoughts from the room across the way, she *knows* that, by a supreme act of love, he has saved this house for her with all the objects inside. He who is omniscient, who can do everything! Soon, very soon she will move into this house, never to leave it again.

Yes! If she is mad it will be no problem for her to amuse herself on her own. Ideas, the most beautiful, incredible ideas start to blossom like jasmine.

But why this love of jasmine? If she were asked her to name her favourite colour, she would respond without hesitation: white!

The most recent anagram she had written was from the following sentence:

When the jasmine blossoms the whole year long (Wenn ueber's Jahr der Jasmin blueht).

(She dedicates this anagram to Herman Melville on account of its recurring monogram.)

If the jasmine blossoms the whole year long,
the whole year long there's blossoming jasmine. So
if it is autumn the whole year long, dear someone, yes!
One would see winter all year long, everyone would revive
his year, every wondrous blood HM.
May rejoicing banish the year's rage in the lord,
who is HM the whole year long. Rejoice when
it blossoms. Yes, brother, yes, HM. When his
ice and blood o woe it burns. Yes, yes, Mr. M.
If the jasmine blossoms the whole year long,
the whole year long there's blossoming jasmine.
You live the whole year long, yes, HM. When he strays
into the fog, all year round — woe, bosom, yes.

Nine years have passed, brother HM, yes. Do you
love knives in your blood? Yes, H. Run, year weave
our liveable clock. Yes, HM, yes. Unite us in
peace while dying. Live, HM, yes. Who
must wait nine years? Everyone. Stay H.[34]

And so it continues, a long litany which she dedicates to that poet who had created a masterpiece from his great longing.

Longing! Perhaps the most powerful dynamo that inspires one's work.

That's how it is for her, because the feeling of "happiness" merely makes her stupid and unproductive. She doesn't know what to do with it.

The next day she goes for a walk on her own. She is searching for a hospital where she had stayed years ago for the short duration of an operation. A female doctor who asks what is wrong with her leaves her short of a reply. She says the first thing that enters her head, so as to leave the building swiftly: "I have palpitations."

The doctor casts her a sceptical look, and she continues her walk. On her way she encounters a group of five small children.

Slightly further on, she sees five riders in a field describing slow circles on their horses. She thinks back to the light in the Hindus' room. Almost everything she encounters takes on a special meaning — it is as if she is walking through an enormous play that is being performed specially in her honour.

That afternoon she is taken by her friends to a junk shop. She walks around it as if every single object had been put on display for *her*, and her festive mood increases. She enters a small, romantic courtyard and suddenly she is standing before an ancient hurdy-gurdy. She sets the handle in motion and while listening to the old waltz that it plays, she begins to weep. The others stand about her in a circle and look on in amazement — until she realises: that morning she had read a sentence in a manuscript that was lying on her table. The sentence was: "And she will come and play the hurdy-gurdy while weeping…"

Had that been a prophecy?

She is then taken further on, to a small gallery. Outside the door is a sign on which she reads the two large letters HM. Not far from this she sees a large spiral. Almost all of the pictures she looks at in the gallery are of a white as cold as marble. She sees nothing but white pictures! As if this were the colour of the greatest sorrow, she suddenly thinks she is in a burial chamber and draws a straight line along all four walls of the gallery with a black pencil in order to enclose both — herself, together with him — for although she cannot actually see him with her eyes, she knows he is there.

She tosses a burning match into a white container whose purpose she cannot ascertain, hoping to see the white man, the genie in the bottle, rise up before her. Then she is led out.

That afternoon she realises that none of the guests she was expecting has arrived for the great party. In fact, it is her host who comes in and asks her to leave his house at once. She is unable to understand her friend's sudden anger, though, because everything she has done seems perfectly normal to her. Then she hears the words "If that's the way it is, you must go to Wittenau," addressed to her like a cue, a signal.

She knows what that means. She remembers this name from her childhood. (Wittenau is where the mad people live.)

She walks out of the house, leaving behind her suitcase and without waiting for the taxi that has been called for her, she takes a tram to the district around Tauentzienstrasse in search of a boarding house where she can rent a room.

When asked whether she has any luggage, she answers that her friends will be sending on her cases shortly, forgetting that they have no idea where she is.

She seems to make a completely normal impression on the proprietress, for she is given a friendly welcome and a room. She pays a week's rent in advance, has a bath and lies down in bed. How will she begin her new life in Berlin? She ponders the question and sees no alternative but to resume writing short stories for the newspapers. Yes, that would be a possibility — she had earned her money that way for a number of years before going to Paris. She is not afraid. She experiences one of her rare periods of courage; she can succeed in anything she wants.

So the problem is solved.

Her lack of cares, the joys of a new life in her beloved Berlin give her a healthy appetite, so she goes out to a restaurant.

Night has fallen. Since childhood she has suffered from a poor sense of direction. Even if she has taken the same route ten times, she loses her way on the eleventh.

She has an ingenious idea: she will let herself be guided. Back on the street, she addresses silent questions to him and receives his answers straight away. He gives her clear and concise directions on how to get to the Zoologischer Garten district near the main station. In her head she hears: "Straight on… turn right at the corner… straight on again… now left… stop!"

She looks up and finds herself directly in front of the entrance to the restaurant she was looking for. Her face is radiant with delight at this communication at a distance. She *knows* that he is unfamiliar with this city, so she is all the more amazed at his truly supernatural powers. As she crosses Joachimthaler Straße she feels the presence of a man from Paris: she takes a quick look and realises it is Man Ray. Is he somebody who has been charged with acting as a *witness* and observing this marvellous attempt at remote suggestion?

In the restaurant — Aschinger's, which she has frequented for years and where one can eat well at very little cost — her enormous hunger disappears and she simply orders tea and cigarettes.

While she is buttoning her coat ready to depart, the French steward from Frankfurt Airport appears and bows silently before her. Another "witness"? She is certain of it — how else could he be able to answer her question with the correct letters of the alphabet and the all-important numbers?

For a moment she has the idea that this attempt at remote hypnotism — for which she has become the medium — has been made public, yes, that perhaps there are people in every city who have heard about it, and that its success is being reported. Then for the first time she is beset by megalomania. By the highly pleasant feeling of being at the centre, an impression previously quite unknown to her, for she is the shy sort who prefers to remain in the background.

On leaving the restaurant she hands the waiter a large tip and departs with the words "Happy birthday and many happy returns."

She receives the same smile from the employees as she had seen in the shops earlier when she had distributed money with her good wishes. She is like her Uncle Falada who, as a young man, had given away his money to passers-by on the large Elbe Bridge in Dresden. (He spent the autumn of his life in the psychiatric hospital in the Weißer Hirsch district, high above Dresden.)

As she returns to her guesthouse she allows herself to be directed once more by the voice within, telling her the way. She lies down on the bed in her room and, as for several nights previously, is unable to sleep. Suddenly the stove starts to emit smoke — the smell gives her the impression that an unknown, shady and disreputable surgeon is preparing to conduct a hideous operation on her which she must at all costs escape. She leaves her room, crosses the corridor and opens the first door. The room is empty.

The feeling that "visitors are coming" begins anew.

This time she expects three or four famous chess-players from Paris to visit her in this unfamiliar room: Man Ray, Max Ernst and Marcel Duchamp.

Just as later she is ready to call the white-coated doctors "gods," she believes that these old men whom she is expecting are secret kings.

But no one arrives. It is necessary for her to light a fire in the stove. That old game with the white smoke, from which the figure of the white man will appear. Without knowing why, she puts an alarm clock and a wallet she has found in the stove. But the fire won't catch. She opens the wardrobe and realises from the things inside that this room belongs to a young man. She puts on his dark blue "steward's" jacket and, dressed in this uniform, feels the desire to travel, to leave Berlin by plane and return to Paris.

Each idea gives way to a new one. Despite unmistakable labour pains, she had been unable to bring Berlin once more into the light of day. She forgets about it — just as she forgets almost everything which only five minutes before had seemed incredibly important. She now wants to leave the room and go to the airport. But she finds it impossible to open the door. Has she been locked in?

Childish and romantic as always, she makes three deep, ceremonious bows before the door and speaks the old formula from the *Thousand and One Nights*: "Open Sesame!"

But the door will not open, and she continues repeating her little ceremony until she is exhausted. In vain! She cannot leave the room. In a sudden fit of rage she throws a vase through the glass pane of the door in order to climb through the hole into the corridor. The glass breaks with a deafening noise — somewhere a door opens and an old man, woken from his sleep and startled half to death, appears at the room. He stares at her, like some ghost. It is the owner of the guesthouse, whom she has not yet met. He calls the police. Shortly afterwards two policemen appear who check her papers and tell her to leave the place at once. She pays for the broken glass with the last of her money and goes out into the street. It is night. She takes a few steps, sees a letter box and puts her passport into it. She waits beside the letter box with the feeling that someone will come — an "emissary," for "they" know that she is in difficulty. And somebody does appear: a young man. He asks her if he can be of any help. What does she tell him? She is unable to recall later. He accompanies her to Zoologischer Garten railway station and takes her to the organisation there which provides the homeless with a bed for the night.

She thanks him and asks him to draw a small black sun in her notebook as a sign that he is a sort of guardian angel. He does so and disappears.

She is now in a room in which several women and children are sleeping, and for a while she loses her bearings: she thinks she is on an aeroplane and about to fly back to Paris. The noise she takes to be the aeroplane's engines is in fact the sound of trains leaving and entering the station.

Unable to sleep, she gets up and walks out into the street.

An old man appears by her side in the dark and she asks him: "Who are you?"

He gives her an astonishingly simple reply: "I am a person."

He speaks these words so slowly and with such emphasis that she is not quite sure whether he says "person" or "parson." He invites her to come with him and, quite trusting, she accompanies him to his flat which, apart from the kitchen, is quite empty. He tells her that he has been unable to sleep since his wife died and so goes out walking at night. He says that this is his last day in Berlin, that tomorrow he will leave the city for ever.

This person, in whose kitchen she spends the night, is calm and friendly. He offers her tea and bread, and they chat like old friends until dawn. He tells her during their conversation that he is a policeman who has been pensioned off because of his age. He does not seem to notice her abnormal state for even a moment. Day breaks. Suddenly she seizes his glasses and throws them out of the window. He starts to wail and reproach her, for he is almost blind without them. She explains to him warmly that he has already seen enough during his long life, and that now, knowing everything, he has no need to see any more. And then she says farewell and descends the stairs. But this old policeman is suddenly concerned. He senses that something is wrong with her. As if suspecting that she has stolen something, he rushes after her and frisks her. He finds nothing and disappears. She laughs and steps into the quiet Sunday morning. It is still early and the streets are almost deserted. The district is unfamiliar to her. It is quite an effort for her to waken the white man from his sleep in his own land so as to ask him which way to go. She hears a rather vague reply: "Straight on." So she goes that way until she hears the word "stop."

Looking up she finds that she is standing before the open door of a church. She enters hesitantly but does not know what she is supposed to do there. The church is full of people listening to a preacher.

Her arrival seems to cause a stir — as if she had been expected. Everyone looks at her. The preacher pauses. Has she done something unusual? She cannot say. All these eyes looking in her direction are embarrassing. She leaves. Without asking him the way this time, she sees that she is near a large black square on which coal is stored. Drawn by the gloomy isolation, she strews six of her white paper handkerchiefs here, as if wishing to leave special signs, a white trail for someone who later will come to confirm that she has passed this way. This too is like a game. And she continues the game by going in search of the *Attic Pretenders*.[35] They must be somewhere, these characters from a novel by Ernst Kreuder that she has read, and who have come to life in order to please her — she is quite convinced about that. She enters various buildings and climbs up to the attic in each one. Some of the attic doors are locked. Only one is open. She finds crates and old furniture —all the typical junk that tenants store away there. She peers into each storeroom, thinking that at any moment she will encounter the characters from the novel. She does not find anybody and returns to the street.

Perhaps they have hidden themselves in the cellar for fun? She descends a dark, filthy staircase and finds herself in front of a large, hot stove. She opens the door of the stove and looks at the fire. With a sob she casts a white paper handkerchief into the blazing coals and returns to the street. She feels abandoned. She needs people. Who was it who had almost never stopped making lovely promises of a big party ever since she had arrived in Berlin. She had lived in a state of expectancy ever since. She comes across an empty late-night bar. She enters. There is no one inside except for a pale man who is placing chairs on the tables. She sees a telephone. And she dials the number 9 three times. She will phone 999[36] — as if this would connect her with the centre where the great hypnotist sits. But the number 999 responds with the ceremonious sound of nothingness, that sound you hear inside a shell when you hold it to your ear. And the man behind his chairs begs her to leave the bar at once. She sees that he is afraid of her.

She steps onto the street and does not know which way to go. She is sad. Her lovely, flying gait has deserted her. Lack of sleep and food have made her weak. Which way should she go, which way? She must find somewhere to rest. She walks and walks until she is standing once again in front of Zoologischer Garten station. She sees the open door of a hairdresser's inside the station and without a penny in her pocket has her hair washed in order to rest. As always, having her hair done is like a small celebration for her. Only after it has been washed will she be able to find again her childhood face in the mirror. And then — her hopes revive — perhaps the party will take place today after all? When asked for the six marks fifty for the shampoo, she replies very calmly that she has forgotten her money. The police are called at once because she is unknown here and the owners are suspicious. What can she do to make these people laugh? She has never managed to make people laugh before. She places a large piece of cotton wool on the head of the angry proprietress, blesses her, and announces that she is the "Holy Ghost."

Then she hears a man who is paying a bill at the cash desk saying to the proprietress: "Can't you see that the woman's crazy?"

These words make her stop to think, and she asks herself whether it's true.

At that moment two policemen enter and escort her outside. She sees the police car. She knows that she has been arrested. And as if it were all nothing more than a joke, she turns the red lining of her white coat to the outside and enters the car as if for a party. She is astonished to discover that she is no longer wearing the lovely dark blue steward's coat.

What became of it?

Full of curiosity, she steps inside the large cell to which she has been brought. She is on her own. There are two long benches set opposite one another, and bars on the large window. She lies down on one of them and relaxes. She remains like this for a long time without moving. She has no fears, but she is very thirsty. She rings the bell and a policeman enters who politely asks her what she wants. She asks for some water. He returns with a beaker of water and, standing on tip-toe, she pours the contents over the giant policeman's lovely cap.

He raises his fist to knock her out, just as he has been taught to do when attacked, but he halts his swing in the nick of time and leaves. She starts to sing, dance and whistle in order to pass the time. Then the policeman pokes his head round the door and calls: "What sort of person do you think you are — assuming you really *are* a person, that is?"

Frightening other people is a new experience for her, and she likes it. But then she hears something: to the sound of caws, grunts, barks, meows and the beautiful impersonation of quacking ducks, a merry band of Dadaists seems to be approaching on the street below, which she cannot see, in order to liberate her. All the old Dadaists she knows from Paris will be coming, and this gathering will at last lead her in a triumphal procession to the long-awaited party. But in reality it is a policeman who drives her to the women's prison. The cell she is locked in is dreadfully small. A bed, a table, a chair. She lies down on the ground before the door and hears the warder exclaim out loud: "This woman is incredible!"

That flatters her. Who doesn't want to be "incredible"?

She is brought water and bread and told to make her bed for the night. She does not move. Here in this cramped room she is seized by great despair and emits a loud cry: "*Quelle vie!*"[37]

The same words come flying back at her as a clear, loud echo, as if another woman had uttered the same cry.

The warder enters. Her face is full of compassion. She brings a sleeping draught.

Finally she lies down and falls asleep — after so many sleepless nights. But the next morning she sees the tiny cell once again and feels suffocated.

She beats the chair against the door with all her might, whereupon the warder with the compassionate face appears and takes her to another cell, a large one which is completely empty.

She tears up her last paper handkerchief, rolls it into small white balls uses them to form the letters of the word *Libération*.

Once this mighty word lies before her on the floor, the warder opens the door with a smile and announces that now she is to be brought before the magistrate.

Why is everyone suddenly so nice to her?

The magistrate smiles, the policemen beside him in his office smile as she relates her adventure in the guesthouse, and the magistrate says to her: "If that's madness then we'd all want to be mad."

"But I *am* mad," she tells the men in the room, very seriously, adding: "I think I'm schizophrenic. I think you must take me to Wittenau."

And that is her salvation. She is driven directly to Wittenau sanatorium.

The director at Wittenau receives her in his lovely room and asks her a couple of brief questions about her experiences of the last few days. While she answers him in a calm, sensible manner she looks out of the open window at a very beautiful autumnal park in the sunshine. The quiet here and the large trees calm her down, and, like someone who has finally reached their destination after a long, tiring journey, she says from the depths of her heart: "Ah — how beautiful it is here."

The man behind his desk looks at her in great astonishment. Perhaps he has rarely encountered a sick person who is so delighted to arrive for the first time at this dreaded place.

A nurse arrives and leads her out. She is as gentle and beautiful as an angel. She places an arm round her shoulders and takes her to the bathroom, where she must let herself be bathed by the nurses. Her hair is washed and she is put on the scales. She weighs 85 pounds, and they are all surprised at how thin she is. She is admonished, she must eat plentifully, otherwise she will never get well. And she is taken to a large dormitory which is very quiet, and put to bed.

Right away she is brought the first medication for her madness. A cup containing a very bitter liquid which produces a strange and almost metallic ringing in her body, as if someone were beating a large gong.

In all probability this medicine is intended to stop her thinking these mad incessant thoughts, but it doesn't work very quickly. Her body grows very tired, and she starts to observe the other women in the room with great interest, and her thoughts start to revolve around each of the people she sees:

Standing right beside her bed is an astonishing creature dressed in a shirt that is too short, and she realises that this being is the first hermaphrodite she has ever set eyes on. He is quite revolting. She avoids looking at him again, but he starts to talk to her. He insists on her accepting a rotten apple as a present. He has spread these rotten apples all over his bed and appears to be playing with them. Their stench spreads throughout the entire room and she feels dizzy with nausea. "I don't want it," she shouts at the hermaphrodite, "leave me alone."

Then he sits down on his bed and starts to cry, he bites into a rotten apple and confides to her: "I'm a sad case, a unique case. The press from all over the world has its eyes on me. I am the strangest case the world has ever seen. They are already writing about me in all the newspapers…"

The rest of his words remain incomprehensible, and he bites into another apple and cries all the more.

Then she looks at her neighbour more carefully and sees that she is nothing but an old, sad, crazy woman. But her story: "I am a unique case," makes her consider.

Hadn't she thought much the same about herself?

It is absolutely clear to her that she is here in a mental hospital for the first time in her life, and furthermore that all the women in the room are mad.

If, therefore, she herself had believed that she had been hypnotised from afar by the famous Man of Jasmine, or his living image, didn't that mean that she had been crazy for some time?

Slowly the enormous appeal of her extraordinary state begins to crumble, that state which she had enjoyed more than almost anything else. She feels sobered up. With a brutal finality she plunges from the lovely heights where she had felt so happy.

From now on she is unable to establish mental contact with him. It's over. As if, on the very first day of her stay in Wittenau she is already on the road to recovery! But secretly she hopes that the lovely period of fascination he had exerted over her will continue, along with his incredible faculties. She observes a woman who is walking slowly back and forth beside her bed. The expression of purest bliss on her ugly face makes her look rather like a clown. A picture of peace. Her arms folded behind her back, she marches along with large, masculine steps, immersed in the most cheerful thoughts.

Her path crosses another person's, a woman whose gaze is so rigid and lifeless it is as if she were blind. She shuffles along with shoulders slumped, as though she were dragging heavy stones along by her feet. A strand of hair dangles on her forehead. She stares ceaselessly at this strand, seeming not to notice anything else. It is agonising. Perhaps she will become truly blind if no one brushes this strand of hair from her forehead.

She gets up and goes over to this stranger to brush this hypnotic hair firmly from her forehead. A gentle gaze alights on her from a lovely pair of astonished brown eyes: "Oh thank you — thank you ever so — how nice you are." She sighs with relief and seems suddenly to perceive her surroundings with new eyes. But in vain! After a short while she pulls the hair back over her eyes and begins to stare at it anew with her almost blind gaze.

Saddened, she lies back in bed and tries to avoid looking at this woman with her strand of hair. But then she remembers a little game from her childhood which had kept her spell-bound for a short while. Like this woman, she too had lost herself in the sight of her hair after she had draped it around her head like a curtain — at first in order to hide behind it for fun, then, and this was the most important thing, so as to see the forest of gold, red, black and brown tree trunks which appeared when the sun shone through her hair.

One woman wept because very soon she would be the "most celebrated case" the world had ever seen. The other was in the midst of a never-ending march and amused herself over something which no one could guess. The third woman was surrounded by the forest of her hair, and perhaps taking a walk in it.

She thinks about the first madmen she had seen as a child. There were quite a few. She has not forgotten them. They left an indelible mark on her impressionable, childlike imagination.

The first was a fifteen-year-old boy. She used to see him when she went to buy sweets at the little shop run by his parents. He sat on a red velvet sofa behind a glass door covered with a lace curtain. He was dressed in black. His eyes were large and black. He held a bunch of small keys tied on a thread up to his ear, making them jingle with a shaking motion. She could hear the quiet "ting-a-ling" through the door. His beautiful white face had a rapt expression. All his attention, his entire happiness seemed to revolve round the sound of these keys, jingling like tiny bells.

People said: "The boy is mad."

That was the first time she had heard this word: "mad."

His parents, who served the customers in the shop, looked revolting. They had gawping eyes and red hair that stood on end. Every time she entered this shop the father brandished his large bacon knife and asked: "Shall I cut off your ears and nose for you?"

They were really frightening because they made such hideous grimaces when they spoke to her.

But she took the large boy to heart and admired him because he looked so dignified. One day in spring she saw him for the first time in front of the house. He was walking round the small garden where the first flowers were blossoming, holding his key-music to his ear. She said a shy "good morning" to him and he looked at her with those large black eyes — with the look of a grown man.

That same year she met a seventeen-year-old girl at her home, which resembled a palace. Her parents were old and very rich. They invited lots of children over to entertain their ailing daughter. But the children, who were supposed to play in front of the mad girl, were almost paralysed by her presence, by her continuous silent laughter which revealed her giant teeth, as she sat there at the table beside her nurse and with her thin white hands grabbed at the small gifts that were spread out on the table for the children.

She wore a red velvet nightgown and her long black hair hung down her back. She never said a word, but constantly shook with laughter.

Like the other children, she was afraid of her. She once saw the pictures the mad girl had drawn. She had attempted to draw characters from her surroundings: long, elongated creatures with enormous heads who floated in space. Was that how she saw them? One night she leapt out of the window, taking with her her mother, who had tried to hold her back.

She had quickly discovered at those gloomy children's parties just how difficult it is to be joyful and light-hearted in front of someone who is hopelessly ill.

She thinks also of the mad woman in the mountains who, as they said in the village, had lost her family in a conflagration and couldn't accept that they were all dead. Since then, she wandered restlessly in search of the departed — and she, too, had developed a constant laugh. With her large goitre, her cropped hair and the wooden cross on her breast, she was so hideously ugly that the children couldn't bear the sight of her and pelted her with stones wherever she went. They often said they wanted to kill her so that she would vanish from their sight.

She also remembers the three people who appeared for a short time in Grunewald, from Russia, so it was said, where an unknown event had caused them to lose their wits.

They walked the streets in exquisite romantic garb, like comic actors in an old play: a man, his wife and their young daughter.

The man had that lovely insouciance of a lunatic who is virtually unaware of his surroundings. Having discovered a new and more beautiful world both inside himself and perhaps even before his eyes, he talked to people only he could see in a lively manner accompanied by gracious gestures. He led the way, ahead of his women.

The little girl's mother swept the dust of the streets with her long, velvet skirts, and was sunk in a deep melancholy. "They are mad," it was said. But nobody thought to laugh at them, and the children left them in peace and admired them, for they looked so beautiful, as if from a story-book.

The local children liked the way these three presented themselves, as if on a stage, and followed them at a respectful distance until they disappeared into a house — one day finally to disappear for ever. Nobody knew where. And the children avoided discussing these three strangers with their parents, fearing the sober explanations that grown-ups are always quick to give. Thus this apparition gradually became unreal and like the memory of a dream.

Towards evening she is given a second draught of the bitter medicine, and this produces a new notion in her: tonight, certain men, of whom she has read or whose photographs she has seen, will appear. Men who have fought for the liberty of their countries, great names like Mao-Tse-Tung, Fidel Castro — yes, even the first Russian who flew into space — and Paul Robeson.

And, if at all possible, the first three coloured men she saw when she was young: Big Chief White Horse Eagle, the pygmy and the Hindu.

Then she writes a polite invitation to a certain poet, rolls it up and finds some string to tie around it. But none of the windows here open so as to allow her to send this "air mail" on its way. She looks round and in the end finds something that resembles a letter-box, a small flap made of brass which can be opened (a container in which the nurse keeps the items she needs while attending the dormitory by night). She slips her message stealthily inside and feels certain that it will reach its destination.

But a nurse, who keeps an eye on everything in this room, says to her with a smile: "That's not a letter box."

But she remains silent because she knows: this letter has already arrived in that other land, and is being read at this very moment. Shortly afterwards she is taken to the psychiatrist, for her first examination. He has a surprising resemblance to an actor she recognises from various films. An actor who only plays comic roles, and she thinks: he has disguised himself as a psychiatrist for fun. Why not?

This impression robs the interview of all the seriousness that normally reigns over talks between doctors and patients. And to show she is also ready to make a joke, she tells him that a wonderful hypnotist who possesses quite extraordinary will-power hypnotises her wherever she goes.

He forces his will on her, and she is quite unable to resist. In this way she has performed the most nonsensical actions, just because he wanted her to.

Then she poses a question to the actor-psychiatrist: "Is there such a thing as hypnosis over long distances?"

He answers this question calmly and earnestly with a clear "Yes!" She takes his pencil and taps it several times against the lampshade which is made of metal. Delighted, she listens to the "Ping-Ping-Ping" she has missed for so long, and says: "And this ping was the musical prelude to his hypnosis in Paris. A pretty idea, don't you think?"

And he nods and is ready to say yes to everything she tells him. But she has nothing else to say. She has already explained everything: it is not she who is responsible for the actions that ultimately brought her to prison and the mental hospital, but he whose name she does not reveal in order to make him seem all the more mysterious. But this psychiatrist, who has no connection with a comic actor, knows this type of delusion all too well, for — as in later years, in other psychiatric clinics — she will be forced to realise to her great disappointment that the delusions of the mad all resemble one another.

Much later, back in Paris, she asks during a short conversation with the white man whether he had hypnotised her. His simple answer is: "I do not have the power." This answer astonished her greatly. On hearing this she is plunged into the depths by several thousand metres. But when she put this question to him, she was, without realising it, already in the grips of a new mental crisis.

The psychiatrist dismisses her. Back in her bed, she begins to think of things from the past — including the war.

Of the bright spring day when hundreds of bombers had cast their fire onto the city, until the sky was so dark from the black smoke that it seemed like night. In the evening, after this chaos, when the streets smelled of gas from the broken pipes, she walked past the newly destroyed, still-smoking ruin of a house and heard a loud, uncanny gurgling noise coming from the charred, decimated walls. Water gushed from a broken pipe into this infinitely sad and despairing evening. She thought that in this solitary noise she could hear the life of her city trickling away, slowly but surely. Shortly afterwards she received news from Copenhagen of a relative who, every night during the war, had seen blood streaming down the walls of her rooms to the floor and tried in vain to wipe it away. (This young woman was taken to a mental hospital; the war had driven her mad.)

A young girl comes and sits on her bed, silent as she pensively studies her two bandaged wrists.

She has long red hair and is as pale as a corpse. The girl tells her of her misfortune in a quiet, monotonous voice: a suicide.

When she had had the opportunity of being alone at home, she had mustered all her courage to cut her veins, and the blood had started to flow so fast and with such force that it had been unbearable, and only then had she realised that she would die if she did not summon help. But didn't she want to die? Oh yes — but how could she look on as her blood dripped onto the precious carpets, the silk cushions and her own lovely dress? What would her father say on seeing his house inundated with blood? So she had phoned the fire brigade, and the fire brigade had brought her to Wittenau. "And now I must pay the transport costs — and the fire brigade will certainly cost a lot — there were four men in uniform. And I must pay to have all the blood cleaned up."

Is that all that upsets her? Has she already forgotten that she attempted to kill herself?

"Why did you want to kill yourself?" she asks the girl.

"For months my boyfriend has been emanating an evil power. It was he who suggested these thoughts to me from afar. And he's a surgeon!"

The last word sounds like a curse. As if only a surgeon, who knows the knife, could transmit such a bloody "command"!

Shortly afterwards the girl starts to speak of her pretty clothes, and then she fetches her handbag and begins to make herself up: "Ah, the first thing I'm going to do when I get out of here is find myself a man and go dancing — dancing…"

So she is already making new plans? What has become of all her despair? Gone! As if by opening her veins she had opened a vent for her despair, as if all her misery had flowed away with her blood. She is healed.

At that moment the door is torn open by a furious man and the girl gets an enormous shock, because her father is standing there, having received news that she is in Wittenau: "So, that's what a suicide looks like?" he shouts at her. "Ha! I have always wanted to see a suicide!"

And he throws her a package and disappears.

She opens the packet and inside it she finds cakes, chocolate and cigarettes.

She begins to eat and smoke. The enraged father has prepared a feast for them. A fat woman comes and joins them, and the cake — which the fat woman devours as if she were starving — gives her such a feeling of ease and trust that she starts to talk about her own suicide attempt. "I threw myself out of the window with my baby," she relates with her mouth full. (Ah, how marvellous to kill yourself and shortly afterwards find you are still alive!)

"But why? Why?"

"Because the father of my child had left me. Because I loved him too much." (And she eats and eats!)

"Aha, and then?"

"Yes, so I jumped from the fourth storey into the courtyard with my baby. When we landed my baby was lying on top of me without so much as a scratch. I also found myself in one piece, I didn't even break an arm. It's simply astonishing. All I did was gash open my cheeks, but they sewed them up neatly for me. You can see the fresh scars here."

They admire both the scars and the woman in general. And a nice fat man comes in and she says: "That's my boyfriend."

Her boyfriend? And the other one? The one who had caused her so much grief that she jumped out of the window?

This boyfriend has brought her potato salad and lots of juicy ham rolls. The fat women hugs him and does not stop eating. How simple it all is!

They hear the boyfriend telling the fat woman: "If you don't get well I shan't bring you anything more to eat. And then you can throw yourself out of the window again, over and over until you're dead…"

And they laugh and hug each other and eat.

After he has left, the fat women comes and joins them. "So where's your baby?" the red-headed girl asks the fat woman. "In the orphanage," she replies. "But I can go and collect my child once I'm better again, and then I'll marry my friend and everything will be alright."

"But aren't you better already?" she is asked. "Oh no," she replies sadly, "I'm no longer allowed to work at my sewing machine."

"Why?"

"Oh, it's simply awful. There are two or three tiny little people living inside, all smaller than my thumb. And when I sew they start screaming and crying in the most appalling way because the needle stabs them through and through. Their crying from inside my sewing machine even wakes me up at night, they are wounded and in terrible pain. I don't know what's to become of me because I earn my living sewing clothes."

What a problem!

"You're hearing voices," the red-head says calmly. "You hear something that doesn't exist. That's all."

"Oh, I'm perfectly aware of what it is to hear voices. I've already had that explained to me. But you only hear voices in your head, and I hear the voices of these tiny people inside my sewing machine. That's quite a different matter."

"Then you must buy yourself a new sewing machine," says the thin suicide to the fat suicide.

"I haven't the money for that," comes the reply.

"In that case you should unscrew the case of the sewing machine and let the creatures out. It would be fun to see little people like that."

"Oh no!" exclaims the fat woman, "just imagine how awful they'll look if I let them out — all cut and bloody — it would be ghastly to see them like that."

"Then you must simply throw yourself out of the window again," the thin women replies pitilessly, and the three of them start laughing like maniacs.

"When I was young…" she tells the fat and the thin women, "I had a picture book which I really loved. It was called *Hans Wundersam*. Inside was a large picture of hell, with lots of devils and their grandmothers. The entire picture was red. And right in the middle of the fire was a tiny little devil-baby. I couldn't bear seeing it because I knew one day it would burn. So I took a pair of scissors and cut out the red baby from this picture of hell. I placed it in a nutshell for its new cot and covered it with a small white cloth. My, how happy I was. It was the only time in my life that I'd saved somebody. A few days later I started to hear a rustling sound each evening coming from the large straw-bottomed chair in my room. I was convinced that two little mice who had nothing to eat were living inside it and that the rustling sound was their sign that they would starve if no one took care of them. So I placed crumbs of bread and cheese in the chair and moved it to a corner and didn't want anyone to sit on it so that the little mice wouldn't get squashed."

"Perhaps you were already mad as a child," said the red-head. "Why are you here actually?"

"Oh…" she says, mysteriously, "I heard a famous poet reciting a poem in my belly."

The other two look at her pityingly — they doubt her sanity. If that's madness I want to be mad too" she said, repeating the words of the laughing magistrate. The two return to their beds, and left on her own she thinks about the night, which finally comes, and looks to see if there is a place between the beds for the heroes to stretch out. She is still certain they will come, immensely tired from all their battles and adventures, to spend a night in the company of the mad women of Wittenau, and rest while the patients sleep.

But the night passes and no one appears. Is there no limit to her enormous thirst for wondrous manifestations? And if something really were to appear, if everything were gradually to change, to become incredible, what would be the consequence? She would immediately enter into conflict with society and be locked away. With the help of the medications she has been given, she has quickly managed to gain a clear picture of the circumstances that brought her to Wittenau. The great enchantment is over. Everything becomes normal — quiet — mundane. Shortly afterwards she has to leave this ward and is taken to the upper floor. She is told that she is on the road to recovery, that she should take her time to recuperate so that one day she can leave Wittenau for ever. This ward is very different, and she greatly regrets leaving the great tranquillity of the first one. She had felt at ease downstairs, where, under the influence of stronger medications, the patients drift about in a state between sleeping and waking. It is always so noisy up here! A mix of patients who will never get out, and younger women who are already preparing to depart.

Everyone seems governed by a feverish effort to appear healthy. If you laugh, dance, play cards, if you offer to help with the chores that are necessary to keep the dormitories clean and tidy, to polish the lino or wash the dishes — if you start to be really active, you are healthy. Then you can leave this place. And there are many here who want nothing more than to regain their liberty and who think that their stay in Wittenau is a ghastly episode that is as bad as being in prison.

She wants nothing to do with these people, she sits in a corner and doesn't speak with a soul. There are approximately fifty patients in the ward. They wander back and forth along a long corridor. The doors, as she only now notices, have no handles.

The nurses open them with special keys and close them immediately behind them. There are iron bars on the outside of the windows. Everywhere green plants. A bathroom, a small kitchen where the dishes are washed, a few small bedrooms for two or four patients and two large dormitories — a ping-pong table — this is just about all she can see.

The only room she has not yet visited is the large room, called the "work room", where the patients are served their meals. She writes a letter to Paris. She explains where she is and asks him to send her books and cigarettes. She receives a swift reply. He asks her *why* she is in this clinic. Over-excitement? And what about? She does not touch on his question in her reply, for it is impossible to tell the truth to this person who is the cause of her over-excitement and probably her entire illness. He knows nothing of this, hasn't done the slightest thing to make her sick. A few days later she receives from him an art journal with the title *L'Infini*.

She translates this word both as "the infinite" and "the unfinished". Both words give her the rather gloomy impression "that it has not yet been brought to an end." In this journal she finds reproductions of unfinished masterpieces, and engrosses herself in the pictures of saints. "To enter into ecstasy with a saint…," was that really what she said to him just before she left him in Paris?

It is remarkable just how little interest she had in the "normal man." His caresses, his words seemed to lack any charm or surprise. What had she been waiting for so stubbornly all her life? What had she expected? Yet the one resembled the other, except for an occasional difference in intelligence. Much later, after returning to Paris, a psychiatrist with whom she is discussing *him*, utters those strange words that are intended to make her stop and think: "He is holy." For the first time ever she hears a man being described as "holy" during his lifetime. She herself would have described him as "unusual", most unusual, for otherwise she would not have become seriously ill from all the years of thinking about him.

She does not even think it has anything to do with "love". Rather a deep, unhealable shock from meeting him, for which she had been carefully prepared by her vision of "The Man of Jasmine".

In reality she is "bird-brained" — too weak, too small to endure a great emotional shock with pride and succeed, like Herman Melville for example, in creating an artwork on the basis of this upheaval. Oh, this lack of intelligence! She is nothing but a chicken looking up at the circling eagle with hysterical admiration, thereby permitting its neck be wrung. She finds them painful, the boundaries, limitations and monotony that are sometimes entailed simply by being a woman.

Day-dreams — without having the ability to express them in an artwork. That's all.

She finds black Chinese ink and a pen and starts to draw on the printed pages of *L'infini*. Later she has white drawing paper brought to her which she makes into a sketch book to which she gives the title: *"La libération de l'espérance est la libération totale."*[38]

When the book is finished she sends it to him in Paris. Much, much later she reads his article on the drawings of the mad, and one sentence catches her attention: "These faces which express infinite tenderness…" And for a moment she thinks of the book she had made for him in Wittenau.

Gradually she begins to take notice of the women and girls in her new environment: the one who is never happy unless she can immerse her hands in water, who washes her handkerchief for the hundredth time each day and begins to weep bitterly when she is forbidden contact with water. "She has a washing compulsion," say the others. She knows this expression but, studying the woman with her constantly wet hands, she wonders whether it is not perhaps the contact with the calming water that the women wants, rather than the wish to rid herself of the sensation of being dirty. She is one of the patients who will be kept in Wittenau for ever, for there is no healing her mania.

She observes another, an old woman who remains a long while in one spot in front of the barred window, conversing with an invisible person in a screeching voice. The medication she is given to dull "her voices" only acts on her body, which is so weakened that she has to hold herself up by the walls as she walks, but her poor mind must continue answering the unflagging animosity of her "conversation partner". For the first time she sees what a torture it is for some patients who are forced to live with "voices".

How strange it is: this old, white-haired woman, already approaching death, finds not a moment's peace with herself. How has she, with her beautiful eyes and fine features, come to end up in the company of such an unpleasant "partner"? The answers she screams are obscene. This dialogue is deafening and revolting. The other patients grow restless — a nurse enters and takes the poor thing into her dormitory. She is permitted to lie down until lunch. But what help is that? She can be heard through the closed door. Her voice is deep and booming. There is simply no rest for her. It is appalling.

Listening to her, one can "hear" her opponent's voice. One sentence can continually be heard in which she repeats the words "the squashed fruit". As if this were the memory of an abortion or a sterilisation. Suddenly her "conversation partner" appears to suggest a new topic. She seemingly answers questions, and now her voice changes completely. She explains precisely the ingredients for a cake recipe with love, patience and epicureanism. There is a general sigh of relief. But in the evening, when all the patients are lying in their beds awaiting sleep after a long day spent in tedium, she starts screaming again, and the topic has something outrageous and horrifying about it: she appears to be conjuring up days long past, events that occurred here, behind the walls of the Wittenau mental hospital.

She speaks in particular of the cellars beneath the many buildings in which patients have been housed for decades.

Hideous tortures, she announces in a plaintive voice, have been conducted on the patients in the cellars, boiler rooms and bathrooms —the attendants and doctors were criminals who have violated inmates quite scandalously under the pretext of healing them. This "report" is so disquieting that the other women listen in horror before finally calling the nurses for help. After an injection the old woman gradually calms down and falls asleep. It is not surprising when a patient gives voice to sudden "impressions" like this, because "something clings to these walls," and such is the appalling form which this sickness can assume. It is not rare for the attendants and nurses themselves to succumb to a kind of hysteria when they struggle to subdue some of these obsessed patients.

The patients are woken at seven in the morning. At eight they congregate in the large work room for breakfast. After that they work until lunchtime.

They knit pullovers for the patients, darn the men's socks and do embroidery work — that is all.

Darning socks requires the least intelligence — the darners form a group of their own and feel they are looked down on by the knitters and embroiderers. Twice a week a pair of imbecilic men arrive carrying a giant basket full of the men's ragged socks and take away the repaired ones. Whenever they arrive they crane their necks, as do the women, to get a look at one another. Apart from the doctors, these are the only men one ever sees here.

The next day she receives two French books from him in Paris. A famous book — "softer than the smoke of a cigarette" (*Plume*)[39] — and another that describes the adventures of a young man who succeeds, in a mysterious yet intense way, in inhabiting the body and mind of his lover while remaining invisible to her.

She really loves this theme and believes, on the basis of her own experience, in the possibility of inhabiting another body in this "pneumatic" fashion. (And the theme is an old one.)

She is sent cigarettes from Paris — her sole consolation here is smoking. She can smoke in a tiny toilet, sitting on the closet lid, and for as long as a cigarette lasts she has the feeling of "being at home" — a free person.

During a brief moment of courage she asks the doctor to be discharged from Wittenau. What is the point in her staying here? All her strange manifestations have disappeared. She is able once again to sleep and eat.

But the doctor explains that she is still not permitted to leave because she was brought here by the police after an attempted fraud, and that is a crime in the eyes of the law. She recalls the embarrassing scene at the station hairdressers. Fraud!

Ha! Hadn't she bestowed an honour on the hairdresser by deigning to let him wash her hair? But at that time she had been enveloped in the beautiful aura of her megalomania. That is now a thing of the past.

A police car with barred windows fetches her from Wittenau and takes her to prison. She is locked in a cell where she has to wait many hours before she is brought before the judge. She does not quite understand why. She sits in the cell from nine in the morning till four in the afternoon, whistling so as to while away the time — but not daring to sing or dance. She must appear normal, or else everything will become even worse than before. The warder opens the door and pushes a bowl of pea soup inside. He disappears.

In the afternoon she at last finds herself in an office, but understands nothing of what is said to her. Are they trying her for fraud? It would seem so. She asks this new judge when she can expect to be released from Wittenau, and he says that they have decided to keep her there for four months.

But she is also told that the date of her release depends on the doctors' decision.

Back in Wittenau she demands to speak with the doctor at once. She repeats her request to be released forthwith. He gives a cautious reply. She tells him that right now she has the courage to start a new life outside, that she is once again able to read and draw, and fears that she will lose her courage if she remains locked inside Wittenau for months on end. She is well aware of how seldom such signs of optimism manifest within her. In vain.

The next morning she joins the sad group of darners and folds her hands on her lap. A black depression edges slowly towards her. When previously she had heard the word depression, when she had observed friends in such states, she had failed to grasp what exactly this word meant. She has known melancholy since her childhood, but not depression. Day by day she grows increasingly unable to do any work or to converse with the other patients. Even her thoughts seize up. It is impossible for her to remember those who have impressed her so as to draw inspiration from their example.

Impossible to think back to the richness of the books she has read and so loved, or the music. Her mind has ceased to work. A complete standstill.

The doctors invite her and the other patients to take part in a therapy called "autogenic training". For this it is necessary to lie on the floor and for the light to be dimmed. The doctors speak certain sentences in a somewhat evocative, inveigling manner and the patients are supposed to internalise them like a gospel and act accordingly. She is told to "relax her right arm, let it become heavy" — then the same with the left arm, the right leg — whereby the patient should feel a soothing warmth and an increasing tiredness in her limbs and finally her entire body. Finally the doctor talks about the solar plexus, which is also to participate in this exercise by beginning slowly to "glow"…

Ah, the solar plexus. The one thing she likes about all this is hearing that lovely word spoken. She lives in great harmony with her solar plexus. It has always been the one part of her body which reacted when she encountered the things that were of importance to her, and she has always been able to rely on this reaction. It always started to get warm and radiate whenever she encountered the music, the people, the books, the art objects, indeed all the things that were necessary for establishing her inner kingdom throughout her life. One could say that while she had hardly ever let herself be guided by her head, she had certainly obeyed this clear response from her solar plexus. And they wanted to "train" it — as if they had come up with a new invention?

She does the training out of politeness to the doctor, but she feels no warmth, no radiance or vibration — for one cannot simply "conjure it up."

She is given intelligence tests, like the others: she is given a page with the beginning of a story that breaks off in mid-sentence and told to continue the story and bring it to its conclusion. She amuses herself for ten minutes by turning it into a crime story.

She is given several sheets of paper printed with certain figures which she is to elaborate into proper drawings, and that is child's play. These short tasks restore a tiny part of her courage for a few moments.

She is shown reproductions of various pictures and drawings and asked for her comments.

"What is that woman thinking there on the staircase in front of the closed door?"

"What does the man intend to do with the hammer he is holding?"

She gives some answer or other without making any effort, but they are satisfied. When shown a picture of a woman who is leaning far over the railings of a bridge in order to look at the black river that flows by far below, she is careful not to say that this woman feels the desire to leap into the water and drown herself. They are trying to lead her into a "trap" with her answer, but it is far too easy to spot. The doctor would immediately decide that she was entertaining thoughts of suicide. So, blushing, she says: "The woman is looking out for the little ship which soon will be coming up-river. Sitting in the ship is her husband, a fisherman, who she expects home for supper." This pleasing response, with its positive approach to life, is met with great satisfaction. And she is dismissed. But she thinks: "If only there was someone here who would tell me what to do, someone with patience and intelligence who would encourage me to devote myself more intensely to something that would bring me joy — perhaps — perhaps I would then escape this depression and be saved."

But there is no one, nobody whose authority she respects, nobody who could rekindle her abilities which she has allowed to decline so much — fair enough then — she remains in her corner — no longer raises her eyes even to study her fellow sufferers — and sinks further and further into total apathy.

That same day the head doctor summons her for a brief talk. "I've been looking at your drawings and the stories you wrote for the newspapers. Quite frankly we don't really know how to treat you. You're a special case, quite out of the ordinary here." "Then I ask you with all my heart to discharge me from Wittenau as soon as possible," she pleads — trying to appeal to him — so that in what is perhaps her last possible moment of hope she may attempt to work outside and earn some money.

"You've already been told that it is not yet possible to discharge you."

What is she to make of this answer — this contradiction? She gives up. She realises that if she remains here for another few months she will become apathetic and despondent. She abandons all hope. This, her worst period ever, comes shortly before Christmas. She is called away from the men's socks — which she cobbles together automatically with a length of wool until the giant holes pucker up — because she must paste pieces of silver and gold paper together to make stars for the Christmas trees, along with most of the other patients. Here in this room which she begins to hate, which is called the "work room", they produce the Christmas decorations for the entire hospital. The radio is turned on and they listen to old Christmas carols which they all know from their childhood. She goes out to the toilet and smokes, sitting on the lid. And she looks for a bottle, smashes it and places the sharpest splinters in her pocket.

They come looking for her and call her back to the work room. She must paint the dried acorns and their tiny twigs, or whatever they are, which the patients have gathered that autumn in the park, with red, blue and green paint for Christmas decorations. It seems that she is being closely watched to ensure that she constantly remains in the work room: that afternoon she and several others are told to draw little seasonal pictures on small white cards, which will be placed next to the patients' plates on Christmas Day. Slowly this Christmas is becoming sheer hell for her!

That evening she goes to bed with her glass splinters. For several weeks now she has been allowed to occupy one of the very few two-bed rooms. She shares this room with a young woman who is undergoing morphine withdrawal here in Wittenau. After waiting until her room-mate has fallen asleep, she attempts to slit open her veins. There is no possibility of her succeeding: she hasn't the slightest idea where she should cut her wrists, and the glass splinters are not sharp enough. She keeps cutting away and actually feels her blood pouring out. She is enveloped in darkness and the wounds seem sufficiently deep to her, she is almost convinced that, after she has fallen asleep, her body will have been emptied of its blood by morning. She pictures how she will be found dead in her bed the following day — how her blood will finally be seen *streaming* under the door into the corridor — and falls asleep with this pleasant picture in her mind, to wake the next day in her bloody bed. "Yes, if only I'd had a razor blade…"

She gets up and speaks to a nurse, an old woman who is very friendly and who is not particularly surprised at her attempt the previous night. "It's not that easy to die," that's all the nurse says. So she is injected with a strong sedative and informed that she must leave her room and this ward at once and be transferred "to the watch room", the dreaded Ward B.

Ward B is a threat that hangs over all the patients who do things that are not normal, or are forbidden. This ward is used to intimidate sick women as if telling off disobedient children: I'll call a policeman, or the bogeyman will come and get you. She has seen women turn pale with fear when the doctor threatened: "You'll be sent to Ward B straight away."

She is led through two doors which are locked immediately behind her, and taken to her new bed in the watch room, so called because there are always several nurses keeping constant watch. The patients are not left for a second without supervision. A doctor visits her and inspects her lesions. The wounds are not dangerous. The doctor addresses her ironically: had she really believed she could kill herself with a piece of glass from a bottle? She feels really ashamed that she is not dead. But how, how are you to kill yourself in Wittenau, if you are intent on doing so? There are no hooks in the walls, not a single length of rope. The windows are all barred. There is not a razor blade to be found. What had she hoped for from this foolish deed, whose success she had probably not believed in herself? A kind of "illness" that compels her to stay in bed! As she notices later, a number of women in the watch room simulate "illnesses" in order to find salvation in bed. As a last escape from a life which for many here has lost all meaning, they come up with a bout of rheumatism that lasts for weeks, or a case of influenza, or if they are sufficiently hysterical, a genuine fever, and allow themselves be nursed. But the doctors are familiar with these fake illnesses and the nurses are quick to chase the malingerers out of bed. Even in this ward, which is devoted to hopeless cases, they want the patients to behave like active people — to continue performing their interminable walks up and down the long corridor year after year, or at least to remain seated, upright and sensible on a chair.

But she lies in her bed and resolves to remain like that.

What she has seen in passing, while walking along the corridor outside, seems quite hopeless. And what she sees inside the watch room seems equally so. She draws the covers over her head and does not move. Then the covers are removed and she looks up into the angry face of a very young nurse from the other ward who, full of rage, says: "I was on duty that night when you tried to kill yourself. I'd be sitting in prison now if you'd managed it. We're decent people here. Decent people don't kill themselves, do you understand?"

Decent people don't kill themselves?

There is never any quiet in the watch room. Patients scream and scream and scream. For some it's their only occupation. One woman defends her imaginary houses from an enemy invasion: "Get out of my houses! Leave my houses at once! Get out! Outtt!"

She has a man's voice — she looks like an old man — her face is hard and brutal. She has no peace of mind. How many years has she kept uttering the same cries — and how much longer will it go on? For ever!

The nurses ask her how "her lord" is in order to distract her. She points upwards and replies: "He's out taking a walk." And we can actually hear heavy footsteps up above — or is that just imagination? "And what are you going to cook your lord for lunch today?" the nurses ask so as to please her. "Roast pork with red cabbage," the woman replies. "Get out of my houses, out!"

And this is repeated every twenty minutes. Would it ever be possible to stop hearing it after spending perhaps ten years in the watch room? And then the others — ah, the others are yelling something else and are completely wrapped up in their shouts. Everyone here is their own alter-ego. They don't speak with one another. Perhaps they don't even see anyone else?

Almost all of them are old. During the four weeks she spends in the watch room she witnesses the death of three women. Oh, it takes time, a great deal of time. The old woman opposite her, for example, who no longer opens her eyes and who speaks French "with someone" in a soft, dreamy, very peaceful voice. What fine features, what wonderful hands, so beautiful now that she is old and about to die, what noble, gracious gestures she makes in the air with her hands. She seems to be happy. It is almost impossible to make out what she is saying, but her voice conveys peace and memories of lovely experiences. And her voice remains in this room long after she has been wheeled out. She is dead. Her bed has been covered with fresh sheets and already awaits the next patient. But the others keep looking at this empty bed as if she were still there — her long, incomprehensible but ever so gentle tale knows no end and keeps floating mysteriously above her place. The patients do not sleep for long in this room. It is never dark inside. Two nurses keep watch, so they also never have time to themselves. Nor does the screaming cease at night. For a few short hours there is nothing but the sound of breathing. But sometimes an old woman, seized by the fear of encroaching death, will get up in the hope of escaping it. Too weak to take even a few short steps, she falls to the floor — and has to be picked up by the nurses and brought back to her bed, numerous times every night. She watches as the last medications are injected into the abraded skin of these women who are scarcely able to leave their beds. "I want to die, let me die!"

No, they are not allowed to die until every attempt has been made to keep them alive. Even the nurses look despairingly to heaven at the sight of the enormous wounds into which they must stick their needles. But *where*, where is God? It seems crazy to her to waste even a single thought on God in this place.

Ah, *that*, that is truly a thing of the past!

A very young girl is brought to the watch room, still almost a child. Like a bird, she keeps fluttering out of her bed, away from this new, unfamiliar setting which startles her, for she comes from the country — and flies up onto the window sill in the toilet and hangs by her hands and feet, no one can say just how, from the bars, trying to find an escape. Then she is brought back to her bed and strapped down. She is given injections, she quietens down, becomes apathetic, but suddenly she starts to sing, softly and then louder. A song which scarcely anyone knows.

A song with lots of verses, the tale of an orphan who tries to dig open its mother's grave with its little fingers in order to lie by her side...

She too had heard this song long ago and also been unable to forget it. She and her sole friend in Paris had made it "their" song, and had so often sung it together. She cannot bear it. All the distress at leaving her friend, leaving Paris, descends on her and she calls tearfully to the little girl, saying: "Not that song, sing anything you like, but not that one, please, I implore you." The girl falls silent, but continues singing other songs till daybreak. Her voice is like silver. Silver that has been brutally beaten, sometimes faltering or breaking into hoarse sobs. She goes up to this young girl next day and hugs her: how appallingly sad to be locked away in this room at the age of sixteen. But why, why? The girl tells her that she had recently come to Berlin for the first time in her life. Her parents are farmers. Her brother had gone mad and taken his life after a spell in a mental hospital. She had spent Christmas in the city with relatives and on New Year's Eve — what a miracle — had watched as the objects in her room started to move, how a water jug slid across the table until it fell and shattered on the floor, how her clothes rose from the chair and flew like birds through the room, and how a chair glided across to her from a corner of the room...

The girl describes how she had fled the house in horror, just wanting to get away, anywhere, just away — she no longer knew where to — and later she was brought here.

She listens to this account with great interest. She had observed the same phenomenon one night at her friends' before being taken to Wittenau. But that had been wonderful, had not caused her the slightest anxiety, and she would really like to experience it again.

Later she mentions these apparitions to the white man and is surprised at his answer. He had pointed at a salt cellar and said, with great earnestness: "It *can* move itself!" (Does he also know those states of madness in which the impossible becomes possible?)

She spends a lot of time pacing the corridor with the young girl, who is very unhappy, yet she is scarcely able to think of any words that might comfort her. She walks past the long row of sick, motionless women, and their appearances leave a permanent impression on her. The doctors do not spare a word for them when they pass, for in their opinion these women have been beyond help for years. There is no sense in asking them how they are, they probably wouldn't even reply. One woman has decorated the ugly dress which everyone has to wear here with an emerald green silk scarf. It is hard to believe the radiance that this splash of colour emits. The woman spends the entire day absorbed by it. Her fingers continually toying with this small piece of cloth.

This possession — which is quite unique here — distinguishes her from the others. And motionless, she seems to be meditating in an intimate atmosphere of luxury.

Another woman has a tattered but securely tied cardboard box which she is just as loathe to part with as a third woman is from her yellow rubber cushion. These small, all-important possessions have something heart-rending about them. A green scarf, a cardboard box, a cushion. So there are precisely three women here who "own" something; the other fifty have nothing, nothing but their grey woollen stockings, their ugly dresses, their down-at-the-heel shoes. They no longer go out into the gardens. They are urged to take a walk outside, in other words they were told to do so some ten years ago and since then no more, because they refuse to leave their places; they are dreadfully afraid that someone might take their chair while they are outside. Each chair has become a patient's "private property." That is why they have almost to fight for their chairs when a new patient arrives who is unaware of the rules.

Only one woman appears to really work here. She sits tirelessly covering numerous sheets of paper with numbers; she is doing calculations. She owns all the buildings at Wittenau. She is the director. She is responsible for every penny spent on the patients' soap, clothes and food. She is haughty and domineering — one gets the feeling she counts every bite the patients take, because who must pay for the meat and the vegetables? She must! She jots down the last figure before she goes to bed in the evening, and at five o'clock she is already up "managing her money" once again — a revolting person who everyone hates from the bottom of their heart.

So the patients dive at their food, devour more even than they can digest in order to "take revenge on this 'finance minister'."

Food! After each of the three meals they wait for the next one, growing fat then fatter still, without taking any exercise. A new fatty joins them in a fresh delirium. Four nurses drag her into the watch room. She has a calf's-head, with glasses and a horse's backside; a mixture of sweetness and brutality.

She is tied to her bed by her hands and feet. While in this position she manages to edge the bed into the middle of the room; no one knows where she gets the strength to do it. Nor does anyone understand how they finally manage to give her a shot of tranquilliser. But the medication triggers an erotic crisis. She seems to receive a veritable invasion of men. The four nurses, breathless after their struggle with her, throw themselves onto the empty beds in hysterical laughter. Then they pull themselves together and listen to the woman's ecstasies. And there is no end to their laughter. "Listen carefully to what she's saying," one nurse says to another, "and you'll learn a thing or two." Their talk becomes as obscene as the mad woman's.

Early that evening she is untied and walks from bed to bed looking for someone with whom to say the Lord's Prayer. She is turned away in contempt. No one listens to her when she explains that she must anoint and perfume herself in order to receive "the Lord" — but this "Lord" she keeps talking about seems scarcely better than a pimp. Is she dreaming of a brothel here in this mental hospital?

There is no shaking her off and she no longer leaves the patients in peace; she's started writing crazy "prayers" to her dubious "Lord", in the style of love letters from a pulp magazine, and she hands out these pieces of paper to all the patients.

Oh, if only a sturdy cattle dealer would enter! And the oldest of the nurses, who is also the most tired, claps her hands above her head and shouts: "This woman must be taken to a 'loud' ward at once, this is a quiet one."

But there is no room in the "loud" ward, so she stays put.

She asks herself what it might be like in the "loud" ward and what manner of hells might be lurking in all the other hideous old red-and-yellow-brick buildings scattered about the extensive grounds.

Another patient is brought in, a being who, if things had gone right, would have chosen to be a man. She — or "he" — wears long trousers. Both wrists are bandaged. He is fastened securely to the bed and sobs. He smashed the window in a toilet. The one rebellious act that a patient is capable of, because otherwise there is nothing to smash: the plates and dishes and pots are all made of tin. At last the fat ecstatic has found her "Lord", and there that love occurs which cannot realistically be forbidden in a mental hospital. It carries on for two days until he grows tired of her, until he finds a new love in the form of a patient who has just been brought in — and then rages of jealousy begin, chairs are smashed, patients are pursued and beaten and they tear out their hair — and are tied down securely yet again and given an injection. A quiet ward.

We all know that there are certain rooms here that emit an odour of misfortune, of crushing poverty, and that nothing can be done about it. They can be cleaned and the walls given a fresh coat of paint, but the air of misfortune remains. No beam of sunshine enters through the bars, there are no flowers, the tables and chairs are old and ugly — this is where we eat. This is where we go in the morning while the dormitories and the corridor are being cleaned. There are no pictures on the walls. We eat with a spoon — there is nothing with which you can injure yourself if one of us throws a fit. Here, too, we are under the constant surveillance of nurses. She sits here like we do, rests her arms on the table, her head on her arms and closes her eyes, like we do. There is nothing else to be done. We don't want to see anything, we are sick and tired of looking at this ugly room. We cannot carry on any more, for here you slowly reach the end of your courage. But courage has long since become irrelevant here. And why not? Why not remain for ever? The heavy pressure encircling one's brow like a metal band numbs everything. People sometimes compare others to animals, once they have reached a particular state. How wrong it is to speak of "being as stupid as an animal." Oh, an animal, an animal is beautiful, an animal is lively and intelligent, fierce or wistful — an animal is a god beside the creatures that gather in this room every morning till lunchtime. An animal is wonderful and a great comfort to look at, something to be admired — but here?

That people can actually stop thinking! What a terrible realisation for her, because she too has stopped thinking about anything. That spells the end for her! Something she shares with so many of the inmates.

Nevertheless, the friends who come to visit her from outside never cease to encourage her, and she begins to hate her visitors. She is no longer able to converse with them. She cannot think of any answers when they ask her a question, and is relieved when they leave. And she is convinced that there can be no changing this. What would she do outside? She decides to do something, something that will convince the doctors and nurses that she is beyond hope. But what, what? Develop a "tic"? A physical movement that she will repeat every five minutes, as if under some inner compulsion?

She is incapable of simulating raving fits or attacking her fellow sufferers. So something else! But what in heaven's name?

Her visitors reappear and tell her: "You must get out of here. Try to occupy yourself with something. Make a start at least!" And she tells them that she wants to remain in Wittenau for ever. "I have no future any more. I have become quite incapable, incapable of any activity."

They bring her Melville's *Moby Dick*. Why, why — don't they see that it's all over, that she could read every single sentence in this cherished book ten times over and still wouldn't understand them?

"You must work — you must work!"

And they leave again, helpless, and she hopes that no one else will come and visit her.

Then a nurse gives her something to clean, a metal container in which the syringes are kept. She hurls herself suddenly at this menial task, which takes five minutes, as if it were her salvation. Then the task is finished. That evening she is given a metal beaker to clean, and she is able to do it. She feels a childish pride. She asks to be given other chores. But there is nothing left to be done, so she lies down in bed and listens to the almost ceaseless screams of an old woman who is warding off the voices that torment her. Another woman dies and is wheeled out. Her empty bed is disinfected and a new woman is brought in and lies down in it for years to come, until one day she dies.

What if she were to roll about in her own excrement like that women in the other bed? Would people then believe that she is lost to the outside world and should be locked away here for ever? And she observes how with infinite patience the nurses clean the soiled woman each day — the same scene three or four times a day.

No, they would scold her, treat her with contempt — they would know that she was simulating — for they are already talking of putting her back in Ward A and no longer see any reason for concern. It no longer seems necessary to keep her under constant supervision. So one day she is taken back and her task of darning socks in the work room begins anew.

The doctor allows her visits every day. She is sent out for a walk on the street with her friends, and from there they go to the cinema and afterwards a café. The noise of the city deafens her, but here she is surrounded by free, healthy people. This leaves a certain impression on her. Her friends speak to the doctors. They want to get her out of Wittenau at all costs. She feels a wave, a surge of warmth, commiseration, faithfulness and steadfastness from her Berlin friends. Two of them would be ready to take her in as soon as she is released. Suddenly she begins, with a burning feeling of longing, to dream of Paris and of her disrupted life with her only friend there, Hans Bellmer, who writes to her almost every day and sends the loveliest coloured postcards as if to tempt her back. In her letters she asks him to live with her once again — she wants to go back to him. And he answers at once, saying that he is waiting for her. A lawyer friend of hers in Berlin speeds her release. She is free. But scarcely have her friends fetched her from Wittenau and taken her to their home for a couple of days before her departure than she takes to her bed and does not want to get up again.

One morning when she is alone in this flat she discovers a firm hook in the wall above the kitchen door and a length of rope in the bathroom.

That little drop of courage, the short flicker of joy… has gone. As she steps onto the chair in order to place her neck in the noose, she sees two cats directing their gaze at her and studying her with their large, beautiful eyes. The cats yawn and stretch in all their dignity, elegance and distance; completely indifferent to the person standing on the chair with her head in a noose. She feels ashamed of herself in front of these animals. She goes back to bed and begins to occupy herself with her body in a way which, several days later, proves to be disastrous. As if the rumours she had heard as a child had become true: you'll go blind if you do that, and end up paralysed!

Whenever she looks at a picture or an object she now only sees the top half. When she attempts to stand up the floor seems to slope to one side and she falls over. She no longer knows right from left. When she goes to pick up an object her hand reaches in the wrong direction. Her friends are appalled, they can think of no explanation other than a new psychic disturbance. And after a vain attempt to find her a place at Wittenau, it is decided that she should leave. The doctors at Wittenau explain that they do not have the expertise for a case like hers. She is rolled across the tarmac in a wheelchair to the plane for Paris.

In Paris she is carried upstairs to her friend's flat on a chair. A doctor arrives and carefully tests the reflexes in her arms and legs. They are normal. A long time passes, with many injections and medicines, before she can walk again, and then her gait is stiff and clumsy — it looks as if a robot is staggering along. When she tries to read she sees the lines converge at an angle and get tangled together. The doctor has her draw a simple square. Impossible for her, the four lines do not meet. When she moves her hand she is startled by the motion, as if it were not her own hand and did not belong to her. Somewhat later she tries to draw an animal's head and is unable to place the teeth inside its head — she draws them outside. Her sense of orientation is deranged.

The doctor, to whom she finally confides the origin of this condition back in

Berlin, speaks of unconscious guilt feelings that have probably brought on these physical disturbances. Then the disturbances disappear, all apart from her fear of descending the stairs. In the first days of her recovery she encounters the face of the white man, which she sees suddenly on the front page of a newspaper. A new shock for her, and she turns away from this face which has become so calamitous and experiences a certain pleasure in tearing it up and throwing it in the bin. They leave Paris, it has turned to spring, they travel to the tiny Ile-de-Ré. Unfortunately, here she gets it into her head to write down the story of her illness. Her friend warns her of the possible dangers of dwelling on this subject, but to no avail. She turns a deaf ear to all his entreaties to desist from writing the manuscript. It would be much better to relax her mind and devote herself once more to her drawings. No! She remains seated at her table in the hot sun and writes for hours on end. The sun is dangerous for her. Her crises have always begun in the summer.

Her absorption in the manuscript distances her more and more from her friend, whom she leaves one day in order to return on her own to Paris. She feels strong, full of courage and activity. A German magazine has published a large number of her anagrams. Does she think she is on the road to fame?

Only one single person, namely the friend who just now she has left behind again, is able to see that she has already distanced herself from reality, that she is in danger. She herself feels she has the powers of a giant.

In Paris she finds a room in the Hôtel Minerve and that evening two red initials greet her on the white hand towels: H M. The monogram of the hotel. She lies on her bed and studies the private adverts in *France-Soir*. This activity becomes a mania, for she thinks she can decipher messages to her in almost every one, and in almost every title of the plays and films. In the initials "P.M.U."[40] of the betting agencies she sees a connection between the name of the white man and her own. She even sees the list of horses, which are to run in the various races, as a new sort of poetry addressed to her. The "H.L.M."[41] of the large Parisian bureau for rented properties becomes a personal greeting, a broad smile for her. The exceedingly pleasurable feeling of megalomania, the delightful feeling of being at the exact centre of events, the state of being elect, manifests itself in her.

A feeling of happiness, of the greatest ease! (What gifts madness bestows on her.) She eats nothing but the loveliest autumnal fruits: the blue grapes which she secretly describes to herself as "black tears." How lovely these days are. And how beautiful this night promises to be. As it gets dark, she gazes through the wide open window, through the boulevard of plane trees lit green by the street-lights, and there — at the far end — appears the house of her childhood in Grunewald, like a nocturnal Fata Morgana. Who is it that has made her a gift of this hallucination with his supreme love?

He!

There is no end to her trust in him, her unbending faith in his supernatural abilities, in his great ability to transfigure her completely, to transform himself time and time again...

What a programme he has thought up for her! What a director he is! What a master at staging miracles! The house, permeated by an emerald-green light, becomes transparent, so that she is able to see through the walls right into the rooms. She sees the Indian Buddha from the Rock Temple, the large Chinese dragon embroidered in silver and gold threads on black velvet, the Arabian lamp with its red, gold and green light. But this view of the interior is short-lived; the walls close. A crowd appears outside the house, gathering as if for a celebration, and they all walk slowly up the steps in a festive mood. The door opens wide and they disappear inside. The door closes — the entire house, even the fabulous green light that enveloped it, disappears.

She gets up and goes to the window. She looks out and sees that the cars and people are all moving in the direction of the vanished house. And she? She is not among them. For a moment she believes it will be possible to reach her house if she walked towards where she had seen it, but she realises it would be futile and resolves to wait and see whether he decides to allow the image to reappear. As always on these special hallucinatory nights she remains awake, and her state of prolonged anticipation is full of hope and magic. Just once, and she *knows* that it will be for the last time tonight, the green light begins to glow again. Only now does she notice that the house seems to be floating above the ground, and that the people who have reappeared in order to enter it are moving along several streets constructed in the air, which intersect amid the beautiful architecture of rays of light that rise and sink with a gentle motion. A paradisiacal scene.

The eternal, blissful hunting-grounds of her childhood…

She gets up again and looks out of the window. Down below is a beautifully arranged ballet of cars turning in circles, unlike anything she has seen before. It resembles a carousel, and also seems to be greeting her — *merci!*

A night of adoration, a night dedicated to her! Then something new occurs:

A large, empty and almost completely dark stage appears — not as a hallucination but rather as a distinct image that rises up within her. But why a stage, and why the sudden strong beam of the spotlight directed at its centre? She springs into this ray of light and begins to watch her own self. An unfamiliar music rings out, with the sounds of instruments from some other land, and she feels she has been invited to fulfil that old, hopeless dream from her childhood: to be a dancer. She waits, she listens, she still does not know the opening movements she must now perform, but she does know: *he* is somewhere in the darkness, and he will direct her like a dance master directing his pupil. Whether she wants it to or not — her first finger begins to move, her wrist bends, her hand describes a small, elegant curve in the air, and her dance has begun. She lies in her bed and watches herself. She senses the blurred faces of the audience in the darkness surrounding the stage. They are watching her. She begins to recognise the music which she hears inside herself; knows in advance what three notes will follow as soon as the preceding one has faded. She realises that it is *she* who is composing this music. A double miracle, of "being a dancer" and "being a composer."

She cannot see any musicians, nor any instruments, but, enchanted, she *hears* within herself the festive sounds of a harp, drums, tom-toms, a flute and over them, the large and the small Chinese gong. The music is festive, a mixture of strains from the middle East and from Asiatic countries. Her fingers become five separate persons with different characters, each one unfolding a life of its own, which is far more astonishing to behold than the movements of an entire human body. Apart from those brief summer's days she had spent in the garden during her childhood, when she had performed the most daring leaps and acrobatic exercises with the unbridled joy of a puppy or a kitten, she had always felt awkward in her movements, but here on stage she feels her spinal column turning into a snake. Ah, he really is not stupid, he spares her the din of a full orchestra, because like her he seems to prefer *single* notes produced by instruments played on their own. She watches as her right foot extends to one side. It rises up until it balances on its tip. Her fingers, hands, arms and head follow the movement of the elongating foot and she sees herself rising like an arrow, if slowly, into space. And naturally she is followed by the white beam of the spotlight, and by the faces of the audience as they follow her on her upward flight. Up there, her tight black costume changes and becomes brightly coloured. She opens up, forming a shining star made of countless new arms and legs and necks and heads, she becomes a beautiful, flower-like monstrosity, and, light as paper or like a dying firework, she descends to the stage. The audience seems unable to believe its eyes. They are staggered. No one has ever seen such a dancer. Nor she. Ping — Boom — Dong — dang — ding — the invisible instruments strike up again. He, who is quite certainly standing at the back of the stage, gives her the idea for a second dance which is very strange. Her head disappears beneath an inextricable tangle of limbs. She no longer has a head — which is truly grotesque and frightening.

After a while she is relieved to see one hesitant finger, then a hand protrude from the knot of snakes, followed by the whole arm which, together with the hand, becomes a bird's head and neck, the fingers forming the beak — they grow and grow, twisting into a long a dangerous-looking beak. It seems to be quite irrelevant that the bird has neither wings nor legs. Everybody grasps that this representation depicts a large tropical bird that is walking with a gracious, rocking gait towards the water in order to drink. This is greeted by such enthusiastic applause, such deafening, thunderous clapping from thousands of hands, that she is completely startled and then thoroughly delighted by her unsuspected abilities. She hears the quiet voice, full of pride, speaking to her from behind the stage: "Anyone who can portray an animal has almost attained mastery." And her arm returns to her body and is no longer a bird, and the scene has drawn to an end.

Then she hears his voice once more from backstage:

"The tiger, the tiger is coming."

She sees herself go down to the front of the stage. She sits for a moment in order to meditate. The little that she can recall about tigers enters her mind and becomes such a certain knowledge, such an adoration of this magnificent animal that gradually she identifies with it and feels herself become fearsome. But this role is still very difficult to perform, for she realises that it is not enough merely to portray the animal's appearance and the frightening manner of its approach, but that she must also show the horror of the other animals on seeing it, not knowing where to flee and hide. "The tiger's coming," the voice repeats, harsh and impatient, from behind the stage, and she understands: she must become a mimic so as to portray both hunter and hunted. "Anyone who simultaneously portrays the tiger and the flight from the tiger is the winner, and a master."

Ha, that's easily said — but *how* — how can one do that? And suddenly she manages it, she has returned to centre stage in the radiant, dazzling spotlight with nothing to be heard but the muffled tom-tom as it builds up to fever pitch. The arrival of the tiger is easy, a child could work out how to do that, how to slink up silently to a group of innocents with the aim of destroying them, for it allows only a few possibilities. But when she watches her own body it becomes capable of "transforming" itself into many different animals which flee from the pursuing tiger in different directions and with different movements. This is precisely what she sees, and everyone must surely be convinced that she is the greatest mime of all time.

She asks him whether she, the tiger, should leap into the auditorium and bring the performance to a glorious end. "No." She is given a new word: "Scorpion."

The stage grows narrow, hot and narrow. The light unbearably bright. She turns red, begins to glow, she seems on the verge of burning up. "Scorpion!" This command is repeated to her with a certain harshness, almost anger. She sees herself on a tiny round disk which proceeds to rotate, slowly at first, and then ever faster, and curiously she recalls the ceremony she had seen in an Asian film: the priests putting the young temple dancers into a trance. The girls place their hands on their hips and turn in slow circles on top of a large flat vessel in which "something" smoulders to produce a smoke with an intoxicating aroma. The girls, still children, breathe in the smoke, grow dizzy and partly lose consciousness — until, with eyes closed, they begin to dance with wonderfully beautiful yet precise movements.

But what she is now "being ordered" to do is not a dance but the relatively short act that constitutes suicide: to be the scorpion that kills itself. She sees herself lying on the ever-faster spinning disk, and how her feet and legs grow together to form a dangerously long sting like a sharp pointed dagger, then curl slowly upwards in an elegant curve until its point hangs exactly over the centre of her solar plexus. She lowers her eyes to look at this, her most precious possession, which reveals itself beneath her skin, which has become transparent, in all the beauty of its tiny and minuscule branchings which begin to glisten like silver under her breath, and that resembles an illuminated landscape that loses itself in twisting paths, constantly awakening your desire to wander about it and make completely new discoveries…

How cruel, how fiendish, to compel her to stab this glory with her own sting.

She feels no pain during this suicide, but while watching she is seized by the desperate thought that from this moment she will never feel her solar plexus again: the soft burning sensation, the gentle vibration, the answers and confirmation that it gives whenever she is confronted with something extraordinary, something of immense importance!

She is overcome by sadness, she feels lost and as if she had been killed — but a quiet, ironic laugh comes from back stage, with a few words: "That was of no real significance, just a little ceremony…" She hears these words and regains her calm, and then he leaves her, never to appear again.

Morning breaks. The whole city begins to communicate with "knocking sounds," first quietly, then increasingly distinct, as if today it is not necessary to talk to one another like on normal days. The noble form of Max Ernst with his beautiful white hair appears on a balcony opposite her window. A knocking sound comes from the streets, a knocking from the roofs, a knocking from the cellars. People are sending messages to one another. Has talking been forbidden today? It would seem so. What a nice idea! They knock with hammers on wood, with hammers on iron, with hammers on stone. In every house, on every street, they knock out the glorious numbers, 1 to 9, and everyone, everyone knows their meaning. For: 1 is the noble number of solitude; and 2 the person who has the fortune to live together with another; and 3 the number of children and perhaps the number for certain invocations and for hope?

4 — is the number of the family
5 — ha! is assuredly the number of "secret societies"
6 — the number of death
7 — the number of misfortune
8 — the breathless number of eternity
and finally number 9 — life!

An aircraft turns circles in the radiant blue summer sky, leaving behind a giant shiny white circle: a sign for her!

And she thinks: "What a night! What a day!" Far beneath her on the street a small dog answers her, barking: "Yes, what a day," and she runs to the window and is greeted by sounds of rejoicing, a veritable concert of car horns for her — she who depicted the fearsome stalking tiger! She who last night demonstrated to a great audience that whoever has found their master can have twenty arms and forty legs, can become a scorpion or can rise up into the air! The factory sirens from right across the city — who knows, perhaps from all over the world — raise their howling voices and, full of fear, full of admiration, everyone hunches their heads between their shoulders and arches their backs in order to receive the full weight of the announcement being made in the open air: someone has gone mad with joy at the superhuman abilities she discovered this last night! The bells start to chime from every tower, and a solitary thunderbolt rocks the heavens and its echo rolls for ages over the roofs and into the distance. A child on the street far below emits squeals of delight — a car gone mad backfires with joy — everything, everything seems to have joined her in a frenzy of pleasure, of excitement…

But that day a well-meaning person comes to patiently explain to her that the time has come for her to find a job and earn her living. She is willing to agree to everything they suggest. So she becomes a chambermaid in a *maison de repos* not far from Paris. This house is on a hill. She is given a small, pretty room under the roof from which she can see the whole of Paris spread out beneath her.

Neither the man who drives her to her new job, nor the female director of this institution — where a large number of women are recuperating from various illnesses in a lovely garden — notice anything odd or unusual about her. She seems quite normal and relaxed. But the women in the garden make her wonder whether the sanatorium might be for the mentally ill. Hasn't she spotted a strange and eerie figure among them? A woman with no hair and a red scar around her bald head, as if her skullcap had been removed in order to peer inside her brain — probably in order to operate on it? But she is the only strange figure among those in the garden. Apart from cleaning the rooms she must also help do the washing up.

How is it that the three young girls who assist in this kitchen begin to develop an increasingly strong resemblance to certain friends from her school days? Or are they the daughters of these friends from Berlin?

Why is the large staircase in this house, which sweeps up from the hall in a beautiful curve to the upper storeys, so similar to the stairs in her childhood home? And why, when she enters the garden for the first time, does she see the same flowers, the same shrubs, the same pines, firs and birches as in the garden of her childhood?

Although she thinks she is strong as a lion, she forgets that she has scarcely eaten for days, and being unaccustomed to this physical work she notices how her powers soon desert her. The heat is exhausting. She is pleased when at last it is evening and she can go and lie down in her room.

The plaintive but clear notes of a violin float up to her from the village below. "Don't be afraid, I'll take care of you…" Oh no, she is not afraid. As the moon rises the room turns into a garden: the walls disappear or consist of no more than the shadows of leaves and twigs. A silver patch of light begins to move, like a sign or finger that tries to indicate something: she becomes more attentive. A little light in the midst of the leaf-shadows grows larger and smaller, like the winking of an eye. Light and shade turn unmistakably into tiny people. Two groups have formed, and they approach one another in a graceful, ceremonial manner. What a spectacle! They greet one another, bow to each other — these "people," no larger than a finger, are quite distinct. She sees their faces, even their expressions. Individual figures separate from each group: a man and a woman. The two groups withdraw into the background and vanish into the darkness — into the night of their land, which is surely not to be found on this planet. The man and woman stand facing each other for their very first meeting. Their heads are no larger than rose petals — oh, even smaller. They have eyes! They gaze at one another. Their eyes are small, like the eyes of birds, but bright as pearls. The wind rustles through the tree outside her window. For a moment everything turns black. When the wind has died down again the man and woman reappear, they have moved closer to one another. Their long costumes begin to flutter, and after this fluttering the pleats, the finery and the embroideries become even more distinct and exquisite. They seem on the verge of sinking into each other's arms, and she hopes that the two of them will never have to separate, and she closes her eyes for a brief sleep, in order to leave them alone.

After two or three days she tells the administration that she cannot cope with the work. She feels weak and miserable. They phone the friend who brought her here and he takes her back to the city. What is to become of her? *He* appears too, after she summons him, and he recognises her illness. "Don't be afraid. I'll take care of you!" Such words!

She has spread a number of her drawings out on the bed. He gives her money in exchange for the last drawing she had made, one which she had drawn with him in mind, with the title: *Rencontre avec Monsieur M (ma mort)*.[42]

He takes the drawing with the simple words: "That's for me."

A new reason for her to marvel, to be delighted. One day at Wittenau the head doctor had called her to a room in which a group of students and psychologists from other clinics had assembled, and asked her to comment on her drawings as he showed them to the others. The drawing *Rencontre avec Monsieur M (ma mort)* prompted a discussion, and she was asked: "Why did you cover the entire surface of the paper, right to the edges? On the others you've left white space around the motif."

She had answered: "Quite simply because I couldn't stop working on this drawing, or didn't want to, because I experienced endless pleasure while doing it. I wanted the drawing to carry on over the edges of the paper — to infinity…"

She gives away a large number of her belongings before leaving the flat to find a room in a hotel, wanting to relieve herself of surplus weight. She gives away clothes and books. Her case gets lighter. She works for several hours on her manuscript in the hotel room. But she loses herself in details and gives up writing for the moment, promising herself that on the following day she will recommence her manuscript on the beautiful whiteness of a fresh page. Then she goes down to the street and meets some children she knows and plays with them. She goes with a little girl to the old church on the Place St. Médard, a church full of sunlight — they are alone. They have fun searching the confessionals for a hidden telephone with which one might perhaps use to phone heaven and — who could say? — speak with a saint. They start to laugh — they run about this church as if at a children's party. In her madness she considers it a boon to be with children who believe in the possibility of miracles, like herself. They get on well, and seem to be rowing the same boat for several hours.

A new joy awaits her: a large red marquee has been erected on the corner of the rue Mouffetard, the district in which she had lived for so many years. An astonishing spectacle is being staged with marionettes the size of people. She observes all the children watching the performance. They remain serious. They cannot laugh at the antics of the marionettes, however grotesque the puppeteers make their movements — so the performance must be bad! That evening a play is put on in the red marquee. The audience is select. She watches the actors with a young female friend of hers; she begins to yawn, and leaves.

There is nothing here which compares with the surprise and intensity of a mime performance. And those incessant words, words… as if the actor's very bliss and contentment depended on proving to the audience that he knows how to open and close his indefatigable mouth and make them understand that he has learnt his script.

That night she calmly tears up the larger part of her drawings and all of her texts that had been published in Berlin. The torn paper piles up into a mound in her room. This action — which she will regret much later on, for these documents form a serious and accomplished body of work, the work of the last fifteen years of her life — this action liberates her. The idea of no longer wanting to possess anything, of no longer having to carry anything, of emptying her suitcase! She leaves the door of her room ajar; who knows…

A stranger, a man, comes to her door and asks whether she is ill and whether he can help her.

She thanks him and says that everything's alright and that she feels fine. Still concerned about her, he promises that he will look by the following morning. A new guardian angel? And she falls asleep with a feeling of liberty, of ease.

The next morning, while bathed in sunlight, she tosses her red slippers out of the window. She no longer needs them. She no longer needs anything whatsoever! These red slippers are a warning sign to the hotel proprietor: he calls the police.

She is taken to the nearest police station where she is made to wait without being told what for. She sits on her chair. Suddenly a line from a poem she had read many years ago occurs to her and presents her with an irresistible challenge: "I plant the breadfruit tree." (Henri Michaux)

These words, which had surprised her at the time, turn into a pathetic plea that endlessly repeats in her mind until she resolves to fulfil "this plea" and attempt the impossible: to plant the breadfruit tree. But that is the problem.

Who in all the world has ever managed to plant the breadfruit tree? The horrors of hunger would be over. The sentence is like a snake inside her, which she cannot resist: she looks around in search of some earth. She sees a flower pot on the police officer's desk, and when he leaves the room for a moment she steals a pinch of earth from it and conceals it in her hand when he returns. But where is she to find the seed that will give birth to the breadfruit tree? All she needs is a seed and a handful of earth. Feeling certain that she will succeed in performing this miracle, she finds a minute object of unknown origin on the floor and presses it into the earth in her hand. Solemnly she places the earth containing the seed in the centre of the room and returns to her chair feeling very proud, her heart full of childlike faith. No one says a word. But who — who will water the earth so that the seed will turn into a breadfruit tree?

She is led out in silence, and a long journey in a police car with barred windows ensues. She does not know where she is being taken. The journey ends; she is led into a building before a silent group of men in white coats. What melancholy radiates from this group. Their eyes are filled with a black, mute sadness. Has an accident occurred? Who is the victim? Why is there a stretcher in the corner? What are those leather bonds for, and those sturdy straps? A mountain of straps! She has seen something like that before. Where?

How strange and soft the floor is beneath her feet!

A floor made of a sort of rubber. She walks cautiously on it and tries a small jump. This amuses her. The special flooring catapults her back into the air. It's like being at the circus.

She amuses herself with her jumping for several minutes and feels as light as a feather. But suddenly she finds herself in new surroundings, without knowing how she got there: a door closes behind her. There is a small barred window in the door. The face of a woman in white looks briefly through the bars and vanishes. She is on her own and gazes about her: a strange room, old and without windows. Electric light. The walls seem to be lined with cloth from potato sacks. There are holes from which straw sticks out. Next to the wall is a leather mattress covered with a horse blanket. In one corner there is a round hole in the ground. That's all. A stranger close by intones a blood-curdling song. Coloraturas, up and down, a phenomenal and very pure voice in the throes of ecstasy.

How is she to occupy herself here? She plucks the stalks from the holes in the walls and begins to play with them, and soon becomes fascinated by this game and adorns herself with blades of grass from summers long past, then uses them to decorate her ugly leather bed, as if she wanted to set up home for ever in this room. She blows the dried blades into the air with her breath and watches as they slowly float down on to her in the form of dainty insects. Is she Ophelia, or Gretchen turned mad by her love for Faust?

She performs this lengthy mime-show for the first time in her life, and for herself alone, but later she is unable to recall its meaning or its details. But while she occupies herself with her game in this graceful and imaginative way, it occurs to her that someone really ought to be there to record this mime in a little film for posterity — but there is no one.

Later she cannot recall how she got from this room to the next.

This second room is black. She cannot see a thing. It is cramped. It is hot. She is seized by fear. She is sitting on something, but cannot say on what. She runs her hands along the walls. The walls appear to be lined with leather. She is filled with a kind of panic. She starts to sing so that she will not have to die in this black, cramped solitude. She sings two different sentences, repeating them over and over: "One finds oneself, one loses oneself." And "One climbs up, one climbs down."

She hopes she is singing as loudly as the woman she had heard earlier. Maybe someone can hear her? Maybe someone will come and free her? But how long must she sing in the darkness before she is at last allowed out into the light of day?

A new situation: she is in a large dormitory, in a bed. And at last she asks a nurse where she is. The answer: "In St. Anne's hospital." She is well aware of what that means. She has ended up for the second time in her life in a mental hospital. No feelings of defiance, but rather of being saved. Everyone is very friendly. She is allowed to smoke in bed. She relaxes, and her eyes turn to the person opposite. It is a creature whom she can only describe with one sentence, with an anagram she had discovered in another sentence: "The agony of the universe."

Or to put it differently: "Here you see the universe in its last throes."

She has never seen anyone who seems to be so enormously aged, and so asexual that they can only be designated as "it" rather than as a man or a woman.

And yet this "it" is still connected to the world by a thin red tube. A tube that leads from its arm to a bottle from which a colourless liquid is being emptied, drop by drop, into the veins of the universe. Ah, these people, they think they can keep the universe alive with one drop after another! The head of the universe appears to be hardly larger than a white, clenched fist.

But how has the universe landed in humanity's hands? As if it needed the help of humans! A mistake — a mistake!

There is a revolting smell of warm milk. All the food she is offered begins to smell disgusting. Impossible to eat a thing. She is allowed to take a walk in the garden, and sees that autumn has set in. She sits down on a step and studies the withered leaves. She leans forward and blows on them, so that they begin to turn slow circles under her breath, then getting faster, flying upward and away, borne into the air by the power of her wishes. This too is a wonderful game. Has she become a witch? A small, human breath produces a great, circling wind!

She is visited by the young girl with whom she had watched the performances in the red tent. The girl has remained sufficiently childlike to be able to communicate without words. They understand each other's dumb-show, they begin to play a game with the stones they find in the garden. They arrange the stones on the tables in the form of figures: people, animals and signs. But the girl has to go, so she returns to her dormitory and waits for night, for only at night can something extraordinary happen. Who can say whether someone might not come in the dark? Someone who is tired from a lengthy journey and wants to rest. She places her shoes in a corner. The space in front of her bed is free. If he appears, they will spend her first night in St. Anne's in a long, quiet and trusting conversation ... and she falls asleep.

She can scarcely say how she had been taken to another ward and led up a set of stairs. Another room, another bed. Another person opposite and the same silence as in the room below.

Straight away someone appears with a needle. They want to stick this needle into her vein. But the needle turns into a monstrosity! The needle is too thick, too long, too dangerous — a murderous instrument! She resists! With all her might and indignation. She knocks over the pretty wooden rack in which the empty glass tubes are waiting for her blood, and watches joyfully as the glass shatters on the floor. As if that could save her from the terrible needle. So she loses her first battle with the nurses, for the first time she hears the sound of the alarm whistle which every nurse wears on her apron, and four people arrive with a strait-jacket. A suit made of thick, pale-coloured material which cannot be torn. The sleeves are so long that her hands disappear inside. There are cords attached to the sleeves and on the long trouser legs, which they use to tie her to the four corners of the bed.

A harlequin costume in which a player from the Commedia could perform a heart-rending scene, if only he'd had the opportunity to study in a mental hospital.

Tied to her bed in this suit like one crucified, she begins to cry bitterly. She has never felt such self-pity before.

It is very humiliating to find yourself in a strait-jacket. She is given the gift of an injection and she falls asleep. He visited her then.

"I saw you were asleep," he tells her later, on a second visit. "I was the first to come and see you." Ah, if only he had never come, if only The Man of Jasmine — her old childhood vision which had appeared as a great exemplar at her moment of greatest need in order to save her from the then incomprehensible and highly suspect world of grown-ups — had persisted only as an oneiric picture of great beauty and gentleness. But the appearance of the *real* "white" man — (what else could she call him, when he radiates such an unbearably strange whiteness) — brought on her madness. Yes, a poor bird-brain such as hers can only take so much…

On waking, her gaze first alights on someone who is neither man nor woman. From time to time this person takes a sip from a white jug that is on the bedside table. How come that here in St. Anne's, as previously in Wittenau, she can no longer recognise the sex of those she sees around her? And this jug full of some liquid? Is one given a special water cure here, that finally determines whether one is a man or woman? She feels certain of this in her mind. Grey hair, cropped in a masculine way, may one day grow long and be turned into a beautiful coiffure. But the throat and hands? Might they too become more feminine with the aid of this drink? Because at present they are too muscular, much too robust. With his grey, despairing eyes, he keeps looking up at her, as if begging for help. His face is red with fever. Where will he go when he leaves this building — in which direction? Here is someone who wants to be saved — that much is obvious.

At last she is released from her strait-jacket and untied. She leaves the room to take in her new surroundings, but finds nothing worth investigating. A long, grey corridor. At one end a window, a table, two chairs. At the other, a door leading to the staircase. No flowers, no plants. Several doors open onto the corridor: she opens one of them, sees a very large, silent dormitory and a very ugly room with washstands and a toilet. Women, dressed uniformly in dark clothes, walk up and down the corridor, alone or in groups.

The fat patients are almost all revolting, the thin ones border on nobility. That is the only difference she observes at the moment. Her entire sympathy goes out at once to a solitary woman who wears her long, carefully plaited hair over her shoulders. It is grey and shiny. What secret lies behind the melancholy able to create a face of such uncommon beauty? This woman seems surrounded by an aura that creates a small area of freedom about her which, like a magic circle, no one dares enter. Despite her age, her face is unlined and her large blue eyes have that pure expression of very small children. Her step is young and sprightly. A few days later this woman, the most beautiful she has seen among the patients at St. Anne's, asks her to comb and braid her hair because, she is too tired to do it herself, or so she says.

But when suddenly asked to touch this "untouchable," she shrinks back, almost startled, and departs quickly from the women with a vague, polite excuse. For some time now she has been back in the clutches of her old hope of meeting a "saint" at least once in her life; seeing this woman has given her the feeling that her wish has been fulfilled.

She must wash herself at seven o'clock each morning in the company of thirty or forty other patients. She finds this embarrassing, for she is repelled by the sight of the naked flesh of bodies ravaged by age. Meals are taken at great speed here; the women eat seated on their beds, balancing their plates on their laps. The food is as stodgy as the bodies it is intended to produce: the fatter one becomes here, the more resilient one's nerves. This seems to be the palliative for both doctors and nurses: fat patients!

The same principle as at Wittenau.

She hardly feels any hunger; she steals out of the room with her plate to where with the dustbins are kept, and throws her food away. That works quite nicely for a while, until she is noticed and then a nurse waits beside her at mealtimes until her plate is empty. If she cannot eat, they place one full spoon after another into her mouth until it becomes a torture. Horrified, she suddenly remembers the scene she had witnessed in Wittenau — a woman had refused to eat, whereupon a tube was inserted into her nose and soup was poured into her stomach. Three times a day. This woman had exuded such a smell of putrefaction that it was impossible to be near her without feeling the need to vomit one's own food. Because of this recollection, and fearing that the same torture might be performed on her, she forces herself to eat.

When she awakes in the morning she hopes only for the evening and the dark, so that she will not have to see any more. One evening, she looks up at the round glass sphere that hangs from the dormitory ceiling. The light glowing inside it at night is very dim and comforting. She hears the words: *"Je descends,"* "I'm coming down," as the nurses often reply when they are called down from the floors above.

"Je descends," with these words, and with her gaze directed at the gentle light above her, a "presence" descends as if on very delicate wings from this self-same light. And her solar plexus begins to glow.

People are thinking of her. The unmistakeable sign of an encounter. And it was not *she* who has extended an invitation to this "meeting at a distance."

A new experience, a new chance?

Every "real" embrace dwindles to nothingness, becomes banal compared with this possibility she has dreamed of, has believed in for so long, because it is unique and not spoiled by over-familiar gestures, by words whose expression are boring or embarrassing. There on the other side of the city, "in his land", he is intent perhaps on watching the empty arm-chair opposite, perhaps with his eyes resting on a similar soft light in his own room — ah — she is certain that he has a far deeper knowledge and is more experienced in these "encounters" than she. This is repeated on the second and third nights in exactly the same way, and then no more.

It is only made possible by the words *"Je descends"* and by gazing at the round light.

When he *actually* comes, he brings her a sketch book full of white paper, as if it were a sign of her salvation, and she reads a dedication — something about people who have lost hope but start to swim in the whiteness of these leaves and perhaps find a new beginning with their first pen stroke. Work! As ever, as soon as she sees him his charm is dispelled. With something approaching despair, she repeats the cry she had uttered in the prison in Berlin: "*Quelle vie!*"

And he answers: "*Quelle vie…*"

She really doesn't know what else to say — she looks under the table like a child in order to see what colour his trousers are. It is quite idiotic. He becomes as awkward as her and she is relieved to see him go.

She is given a piece of wood and a small bottle of Chinese ink which she uses to make her first drawings, listless and without grace or imagination.

From now on her friends bring her new sketch books, paints, inks, brushes, pens, and she is encouraged to attend a drawing class that a teacher (Legrand) holds twice a week in a small studio. On her way to the studio she chances on her friend, she throws herself into his arms and feels consoled and no longer abandoned. He comes each visiting-day, bringing her presents, encouragement, patience, infinite patience and friendship. He brings other friends, a whole group of people who help, divert, stimulate and encourage her. He brings books and, every time, flowers. With his help and the help of others the torn drawings are retrieved from the hotel dustbins and carefully stuck back together by a specialist: an exhibition is prepared (at the Galerie Le Point Cardinal).

But she has already half-submerged into the bottomless depths of a new, deep depression, as if that were the rule with this illness. A few unusual days, a few nights filled with the shattering experiences of hallucinations, a short upward momentum, a feeling of being extraordinary — and afterwards the fall, reality, the realisation that it had all been an illusion.

She marches along in the grey fifth column of the terminally depressed. The struggle between her medication and her state of delirium — during this one brief period that had made her madness worthwhile, because it had rewarded her with new experiences — is quickly won by the medication. But managing to dispel this deep depression is another matter. She spends weeks and months in her bed with her eyes closed, just as in Wittenau. She no longer has any desire to wash herself, comb her hair or speak.

The medication is changed several times… in the end she is given one that has a devastating effect (Majeptil): she becomes stiff, her muscles seize up. Like someone on the verge of drowning, she seeks out a point in the room to which she can cling. This point is a small red artificial flower on top of the radio on the other side of the room. By staring at this red spot she can hold her head above the sea of torture in which she feels she is swimming. Whenever she releases her eyes from the red spot, she "drowns". She no longer wants any visitors, she doesn't know what to say to them. But she is not left on her own, people stay at her side and give her encouragement.

The doctors, whose research has shown them that this medication causes a rigidity of the body, are satisfied. She begins to hate the doctors. The depression remains. She is allowed out, accompanied, for several hours in order to attend the opening of her exhibition. It does not interest her, nothing whatsoever interests her. She is taken downstairs to another ward so as to get her out of her eternal bed. Here the patients spend the day, from morning to evening, in a large room with tables and chairs and a television, then return upstairs at eight in the evening right up to the roof, where each patient is put in a small glass cell for the night. It is very pleasant, being alone. And time passes. More than a year has passed. "Isn't there some remedy for this depression?" she asks a psychiatrist, and his cautious reply is: "It may take many months."

If that's the case what is there for her to do here? For a long time she had watched the woman who, in her presence, had unravelled for the fiftieth time the grey sock she had carefully been knitting for twenty years. The sock will never be finished.

For a long time she had watched another woman who continually places five chairs in a circle around herself and flies into a rage when anyone touches them. Also the woman… oh… everything repeats itself here, just as it did in Wittenau.

"What do you want?" she asks her friend, but she allows him to take her home, perplexed, ashamed because she will never be able to repay him for the energy he spends wrapping her in warmth, friendship and encouragement, like a warm overcoat.

When at last she is back home with him and able to touch once more, after all this time, the little objects with which she has lived for so many years, she recalls the woman at St. Anne's who longed like a sad child for the small, pitiful objects she stored at home like treasures: "What will become of my little boxes if no one looks at them, if no one opens them, if no one cleans them?"

"Do you think you will ever be cured?" a psychiatrist asks her one day at St. Anne's, and with a certain satisfaction she answers: "No."

When spring arrives she drives with her friend to the small house at Ile-de-Ré. She starts to work again, and, hardly believing it's possible, she produces drawings of some quality. More importantly her concentration returns, which she needs in order to make anagrams. The proximity of the sea, the sensation of the great depths beneath her feet when she swims, makes her dizzy with freedom, and she has a new feeling of happiness. Obsessed with faces for as long as she can remember, that is what she draws. After the initial, tentative "floating" of the pen over the white paper, she discovers where to place the first eye. Only once she is "being looked at" from the paper does she begin to find her bearings and can effortlessly add one motif to the next. In this way she draws the "family" she has never had and allows them to adopt her. A silent, patient family with small, tender smiles at the corners of their mouths and the eyes of cats.

For the first anagram this summer she takes the line:

The Imaginary Madness (Der Eingebildete Wahnsinn)

The result:

Your ways into the hinterland B.
where it rains in blindly. — Wo —
Woe — Deliriums are prayers. N — N — N —
The wind blows. Entering into
crazed images ends in
suffering. The madness is cramped. Simply
rising, then suffering. Hib! Who?
Him! When? Never! Deluded!

What? Rien! H — D — S —
Suffering begins. Dehi —
Dehi — lively deliriums. N — N — N —
Will it never end?
No G — B — L — I — H — Who? — [43]

It is poor and imperfect. The rule for anagrams is that they must use all of the letters contained in the initial phrase. But here some letters have been left over, which is not allowed.

The next morning she reads in the newspaper that Nehru's body has been cremated on sandalwood and rose petals.

So the initial phrase for her second anagram is:

On sandalwood and rose petals (Auf Sandelholz und Rosenblaettern).

(She always uses ae, ue and oe for the umlauts ä, ü and ö. This provides her with two letters instead of one, so that it is slightly easier to create new words.)

The result, the anagram from this second sentence, is:

Nehru's death changes everything —
— you gentle land —
— sun and basking distances —
— ancient logs —
— gentle, silent women —
O ancient magic land Death.[44]

But this anagram, too, is not without flaws.

She regards these first two attempts, performed after such a long interval, as exercises.

The anagram from the third phrase that she chooses is perfect.

The phrase is:

The Strange Adventures of Mr. K. (Die seltsamen Abenteuer des Herrn K.)[45]

The result:

It is cold. Ravens are talking around the lake. Deer
and blackbird are drinking tea. Raven, seer
of the evil in the evening. First stars. Speak, K!
The first toad died in great misery of
Hik. The donkeys' dream was talking next door. Poor
Mr. K.'s nose bled. Lake,
dark lake of the ravens. Breath means
life, means winding dreams of the
strange adventure. Those of Mr. K.? [46]

She thinks of China and the impossibility of her ever visiting that land. While considering this she suddenly recalls the following sentence:

You will find the secret in a young city. (Das Geheimnis findest Du in einer jungen Stadt.)

She examines the sentence for anagrams and comes up with the following:

Youth sings: now the sea is your harbour — is
dream and the hunt, the spirit's inner-festivities, which
despatch him to sombre, stony days, yes, you. And his
hand and mind have been made immune by solemnity. Yes, you! — victories are
found intuition. You travel to the city of Yim-Sing.
Enter the youngest street and find AMIN the TI.
He says: yes-no-once-never-foe-courage there are... You — DHG.
Secret sign? Jade stone? You find the meaning.[47]

Naturally she is enchanted by this mysterious message, that one should "enter the youngest street" and turn to a certain AMIN the TI, as well as the words this unknown person speaks.

The old, dangerous fever for anagrams has her back in its grip. She creates one after another. This is dangerous, because once again she shuts herself off completely from her surroundings. She does notice as a new crisis descends. No hallucinations, nothing unusual, but people see a change in her. She no longer sleeps or eats, she wants to be free. She explains that she wants to live alone. This desire always leads to a catastrophe and she is well aware of its consequences, but she always forgets as much at the critical moment. Once again a door closes behind her, so gently she scarcely notices. She is in the psychiatric clinic at La Rochelle: La Fond.

No sooner has she arrived than she asks the doctor for her immediate release. She doesn't feel ill. Why is she here?

"First you must calm down. Then we shall see." Such is the answer she receives.

Filled with rage she throws her glasses in the dustbin. She won't work here, won't lift a finger.

What's the name of this clinic? "La Fond."

She turns this into: *Le Fond.*[48]

Is one supposed to reach the depths in this clinic, to meditate and get to the bottom of some problem?

Appeased by this explanation, she makes herself at home in this new environment. She spends the first night without sleeping, smoking in a large dormitory. No one disturbs her. At one point she gets up in order to explore her surroundings. She looks into another dormitory, and into a small room with comfortable armchairs. She sees a staircase and walks up to the next floor. She enters a place that resembles a morgue: lying on the beds are mounds of white, wheezing flesh.

There is a foul stench in the room. It's quite revolting. And yet: how noble people can appear when they are asleep!

But here?

She thinks of a saying she had heard long ago and which seems to contain a certain truth: "It is the spirit that forms the body…"

And she forgets that she herself had been just such a mound of dead, ugly, foul-smelling flesh during the worst moments of her mental stupefaction — in her total depression.

But the image of the dormitory above does not cease to torment her. The next day she sees — or *thinks* she sees — "this flesh" being picked up by an bus which stops in front of the building, and the image arises within her of an enormous oven belching clouds of black stinking smoke.

No! She is not in a normal state!

She is given a small room where she sleeps alone. A blessing. She is given a pretty summer frock. What a difference to the ugly clothes at Wittenau and St. Anne's!

Here at La Fond the patients drink wine with their meals. A group of young girls adopts her as their "mother" for fun. They are allowed to lie on the grass and chat in the shade of the old trees. There is laughter and singing, and cats and flowers everywhere. Why not stay here forever?

She starts to fall into the old temptation: wouldn't it be simpler for her to end her days in a psychiatric clinic?

But she is not left to dream of such a pleasant future, she is summoned to the studio to work. It's exactly the same as the work room at Wittenau: here the patients spend the their time between eight in the morning and lunchtime, and then in the afternoon until six. The women embroider, knit and sew under the surveillance of a nurse. Since they know that she likes to draw, they have provided her with paper and black Chinese ink.

A few days pass before she sets to work. The sun keeps enticing her into the garden. She is allowed do as she pleases, even though that is against the house rules. She is persuaded into beginning work. She sits before the empty white sheet of paper, dips her pen in the black ink, and for a moment that familiar, magnificent feeling of suspense comes back to her: how will the first drawing turn out? What might appear? Just as she makes the first black mark on the paper, the music on the radio is suddenly interrupted and the voice of the white man calls out: "*Je suis fou du joie!*"[49]

After this interjection the music immediately continues from very same the point where it had stopped. The women exchange surprised glances and one of them says: *"C'etait un fou."*[50]

Wonderful! However far he is away from her he *knows* and *sees* that she is beginning a drawing! Everything is possible for him, but she had already established that.

This little bit of magic, unfortunately rather weak and scarcely comparable with the great transfigurations that real madness was able to effect on her, is sufficient to fire her childlike belief in miracles, so that she feels herself to be in a mild, mental fever which provides just enough of the enthusiasm she needs to produce this new drawing. He *knows* that work can spell rescue for her.

The first eye comes into being in the whiteness. It has an evil expression and it summons the second eye with force!

The whole of the devilish face appears over the next couple of days, growing blacker and blacker, and she breaks one nib after another in her desire to make this grimace ever more terrifying.

"C'est le diable,"[51] the others say.

That day she hears a sentence on the radio: "The game of the king and queen commences."

On one side is some empty space, and there, under the influence of some pleasant music, she constructs a Chinese pavilion from musical notes. The king's palace. Oh, if only this drawing would never come to an end. It fills her with the same enthusiasm as the one she called *Rencontre avec Monsieur M (ma mort).*

The doctor takes a look over her shoulder while she is drawing, and asks her to lend him the drawing for a day.

Here in La Fond she is given forty cigarettes a day and, if she asks, two jars of yoghurt. She endeavours to consume only red and white things: wine, white bread and yoghurt. Every morning and evening she embraces a petite, fragile old lady because she has such beautiful blue eyes. The little old woman stretches out her arms to her whenever she sees her coming in the distance. Never before has she felt such affection for an old person. Her eyes sparkle with intelligence — why is she here?

One morning she saves two new-born kittens from being drowned, and these cats, which gradually grow larger, are a source of joy to all. She has never saved anyone before, except the devil's baby in her children's picture book. The kittens are taken in by two of the nurses and given a home. As if there were no cause for misery here? Wittenau and St. Anne's were brimful of misery!

She begins to listen, to open her eyes.

She wakes up! Almost every morning at 5 o'clock one can hear quiet sobs from the floor above, like the whining of a puppy, seeming to get closer and louder until they become a long drawn-out howl and finally a piercing and scarcely human screech. Fists hammer at a door, and at last the tension breaks with the sound of glass shattering.

The screaming ceases, the door with the broken pane is opened by a nurse.

"Who was that?" she asks the others. "Madeleine," they answer. It's always that way with with her.

One morning she walks into the garden behind Madeleine and sees her — a young girl — clinging to the bars of the large gate that separates the women's garden from the large park outside.

Madeleine waits and cries. She sits down behind Madeleine in the grass and waits with her. But who — who is she waiting for in such despair? From time to time Madeleine shouts an almost incomprehensible name.

Suddenly Madeleine seems to try to climb through the bars, which is impossible: someone approaches.

Madeleine clings like a bird to the bars of its cage, repeating a name incessantly. But the person walks past!

This causes her to fly into a rage. She begins to gyrate like a spinning top gone mad, she stamps her feet on the ground, beats her fists on the invisible person who didn't listen to her, she breaks his bones, tears out his hair, she devours him, chews him and spits him back out. This obsession, fanned by hatred, is fantastic to behold. She presents such a clear picture of a murderer that you believe you can see the victim before her.

It remains the most heart-rending mime show she has ever seen, and she asks the others who this girl is waiting for so desperately. "For her sister," they reply.

That evening the same scene is repeated. The girl stands once more at the bars and calls her sister's name. Someone comes and stops this time. She sees, for the first time, two people embracing through bars. Each searches frantically through the pockets of their pinafore to find something to give the other: an apple, a piece of chocolate — it's over. Each of them is called back to a different building from a different side. "Why don't they let the two sisters live together in the same house?"

"They've tried that. But no sooner are they together than they start hitting each other."

Later she learns that the two girls are orphans. No one comes to visit them.

The male patients look at them with commiseration when they pass them in the park. The younger crochets a strip of wool which has turned black over the years, for she dreams of crocheting her older sister a large, magnificent wrap for the cold winter days.

The next morning starts once again with the distant whining of this small, desolate puppy, until finally the pane in the office door is shattered again and the room is unlocked so that she can begin her long vigil outside in the garden. One day this screaming reaches such an unbearable pitch that she leaps up and extinguishes her burning cigarette on the girl's back, directly between her shoulders.

The howl sinks like the sound of a fading siren and stops. Something astonishing occurs: the girl thanks her for the pain, adding: "That was a great help to me."

Pensively she inspects the hole the cigarette has burnt in the girl's pinafore and begins to suspect a hideous masochism.

Had she been blind? On closer inspection she realises that even here there is scarcely anyone who is not suffering. The beautiful garden, the cloudless sky, the women's pretty frocks — a mere semblance of gaiety that has deluded her.

How many "couples" have found each other here but not been allowed to visit one another? The first man she observes is called Jesus. He comes to the bars twice a day in order to embrace a girl. He is mute. But at least he can hear what the girl has to tell him in those few short minutes. He presses his cheek to the bars, so that the metal divides it in two, and receives countless, hasty, childish kisses.

"*Ah, c'est penible, penible,*"[52] remarks a man who is watching them. He is standing a little way off beneath the trees. Yes, it is painful and distressing to see. Jesus's girlfriend confides to her that she wants to marry her beloved and that they first met five years ago at the ball that is sometimes held here in summer for the patients. But she adds sadly that the doctors will not allow this marriage. She is an epileptic and Jesus is a drinker who is here to dry out.

She watches the brother and sister who embrace every evening through the bars and pass each other little gifts.

Every afternoon, every evening a woman falls into a rage in front of her chair; her rage makes her swing her arm in a circle as if she is stirring an imaginary dough, but these motions seem rather to assist the woman in stirring up an inner sewer until eventually a stream of insults issues from her mouth. In this way she "evacuates" herself and then sits down contentedly at the table in order to stuff the sewer full once more with a mountain of food.

Or the woman who allows herself to slip slowly from her chair onto the floor, where she attempts to scratch out her own eye. The eye is constantly red and inflamed. No one pays any attention to her. Who knows, maybe in two years her eye will finally drop out and roll away.

How can one ever forget such images?

There is one woman here — only one — who has the wonderful gift of making the others laugh. A circle forms around her, as if around a second sun, in order to warm themselves and look on.

Her topic is love. A kind of love that allows one to die of laughter.

She's had so many lovers, so many children — it's incredible when you stop to think about it. Off they go into the flowery meadows with a basket of wine, meat, cheese and bread, they embrace, laugh, and then leave one another to find others with whom they can laugh even more — without any problems. "*Quelle bordel, la vie!*"[53] a young girl shouts from amidst the audience, and rolls in the grass with laughter.

Another woman slips away, crying at the impossibility of ever walking through the fields with a man.

Far off to one side of them sits a woman talking quietly with an invisible partner; she no longer notices whether it is summer or winter. She does not hear when mealtimes are called. She is a picture of contentment. This "couple" lives in complete harmony.

What good fortune to find a worthwhile "conversation partner" in one's illness, someone who does not insult or attack you. She thinks back to the woman in Wittenau who spent many hours talking with a small imaginary needle, a needle full of gaiety and amusing ideas.

This little needle always gave her good, intelligent advice.

A word from the man behind the bars, the only one she sometimes talks to, astonishes her. He says: "*On est fou,*"[54] with an almost contented smile.

(As if there were solace and security in madness, which can be true, by the way.)

He presents her with some apples. He works in the park. He has a large, beautiful dog at his side. The women have their cats, the men their dogs. It is good for the patients to have animals about them. There is also a farm where the men can work outdoors if they wish. And once a fortnight the patients publish a newspaper containing texts, puzzles and drawings.

Once or twice a month, a film is shown.

One can go to the canteen and have a drink.

But there is only one doctor for three hundred sick women!

Sometimes she sees a small fifth column of sick children out walking in the park. And in the canteen she sees the tall old lonely man with a marvellous face, so marvellous it can only have been carved by melancholy — so different from depression, and thus tolerable. On one of the paths in the park she passes a sort of "abyss", from which a special fifth column that she has known since her childhood turn their heads to look up at her. These "frog kings", these embryo-faces which live in the light, appear to be drawn to the sun by every fibre of their being, as if the sun could preserve something of this seemingly interrupted process of growing up.

She has seen it all. She is discharged. Returns to Paris. She puts on a white coat and goes out for a walk — into a new black depression which at first she scarcely notices.

No! There had hardly been anything "worthwhile" in the last crisis, hardly anything that could make up for a new despair. Unable to sleep, eat or work, she locks herself in her hotel room.

"I feel as though I am in prison," she says to a psychiatrist on one occasion. And he answers: "You are your own prison."

"I am trapped in a never-ending circle," she says to another psychiatrist. He answers: "I do not believe in this circle."

But both "circle" and "prison" disappear — her ability to work returns, until the next "PING" from across the way, until the next sound of the hammer, repeating those 9 or 6 blows on a roof in its unsettling way. It's all a question of remembering that the "ping" happens when an unknown and unimportant woman washes the dishes, and that hammer blows are necessary when masons have to split a stone… Will this be enough to rescue her?

NOTES ON HER LAST (?) CRISIS

The weather on 6.6.66, a date that seems worthy of and significant to her, is very hot.

She draws the curtains behind her, lies down on the sofa and looks at the clouds through the open door of the veranda. Almost immediately she is fascinated. It seems to her as though she is studying clouds for the very first time in her life, and on this day they are of enormous beauty. She starts to interpret everything, and at the same time to hallucinate. She begins to see very distinct images in the clouds: the history of the whole of humanity parades before her eyes. All the peoples who have ever populated the earth down the millennia appear in the sky. The fact that she is allowed to see this spectacle makes her feel that she is *one of the elect.*

She *knows* that this sight could only manifest itself on this one particular day, for this day, with a date in which the number 6 is so often repeated, is dedicated to death.

Everything that has ever lived on earth, humans and animals, has this unique opportunity to be observed by a select group of initiates. She is tempted to believe in the possibility of a paradise in heaven, a place in which the soul of every single creature that has ever lived continues to exist in a new, eternal and very aerial life.

These souls, composed of clouds, give a faithful representation of the departed, humans and animals, at the moment of their death. Strangely, though, there is no peace, even in paradise: instead, the struggle continues. The various races from the various epochs of history do battle in heaven, maiming and killing one another. A new kind of being issues from their deeply-inflicted wounds, along with *white* cloud-blood that streams across the blue sky. These incessant cloud-soul-births issue from the noses and mouths, indeed from all the orifices of their constantly changing bodies.

The images are dramatic.

She cannot see the upper part of the sky from where she is lying because the door to the veranda is not tall enough. As in the past, she suspects the presence of God in the obscured part of the sky. She feels that she is forbidden from seeing him today. So she sinks deeper into the cushions and bends her head slightly backwards. From this new position, several centimetres lower, she is able to see an enormous hand up above, stretched out as if to protect the earth. The hand of God? Why doesn't he reveal his face to her? The hand turns into the head and neck of a crocodile with one single, evil eye. The crocodile transforms back into the hand, which in turn becomes the crocodile again. She realises that this crocodile is guarding the sky.

She alters her posture once more in order to see what is above the crocodile. She discovers the small face of a very renowned and talented actor, a face that constantly changes. Is God a clown?

The face assumes the features of Charlie Chaplin, then of Hitler, followed by a sequence of faces she does not recognise.

She lowers her gaze to the bottom-most clouds and sees the dead heroes of her childhood pass by in silent procession: hordes of Red Indians! They float feet first. Some are transparent, others very compact and solid. She sees the Jews who were tortured to death during the Nazi era. She looks at the clouds until darkness falls, and she knows that on this day an elect community of people is standing on the roofs of buildings all over the world, and that like her they have been witnesses to the past. Among them, very close to her, is Christian[55] who, accompanied by his noble teachers, has at last discovered his future profession as a Baroque wood-carver, for the clouds today are the purest Baroque.

With that part of her mind that has remained unaffected by her state, she reflects that the "white man" will be intelligent enough to ensure that the images in the sky have been filmed, and that this film will be shown in all the cinemas of the world so as to prove to humanity that nothing that has ever existed on earth disappears.

The next day she begins to draw under his direction. He signals his presence in the house by means of knocks. This time she does not hear a "PING," but instead a hard, hollow rapping noise from the man who is once more forcing his will upon her. Once again he is hypnotising her from a distance. Their mutual work turns out to be extremely beautiful. She has become a medium, the only state of which she is worthy.

She can rest assured that a new signal will be knocked out to help her whenever she hesitates before drawing the next line. This collaboration is full of harmony. The result is of high quality — but is suddenly ruined because he does not stop knocking, and in the end she tears up this precious document in a fit of sadness and rage.

What did their joint drawing depict? There was a clear division between a seemingly dead couple on the ground and a very white paradise above.

Impossible to sleep after such a day. She fetches a sheet and pillow and spends the night on the sofa. The night is short, dawn arrives early at this time of year. From the moment day breaks she expects visitors; they will sit at her long table and begin the Vietnam peace conference. It will be chaired by the writer from Berlin, Hans Zehrer. She had read an intelligent comment from Zehrer in the papers during the period of political tension that followed Berlin's division into two zones:

The reunification of Berlin is not a matter of foreign policy, but a personal matter for the citizens of Berlin. Thus it would be unacceptable for a new world war to be declared on account of the political circumstances in Berlin. She also expects Christian, and lays out a white pullover for him. White! The colour of dignity and excellence.

She had offered to give the white man a similar pullover when he had visited her in the rue Mouffetard, arguing that it was Christmas — in the middle of summer.

Today she listens to her favourite gramophone records, playing Beethoven's

Ode to Joy from his Ninth Symphony over and over again. This time the music has enormous power over her. She plays songs composed in the resistance fighters' camps in Vietnam. She pours a bottle of red tomato juice onto her white bed-sheet in order to unite the colours white and red, because she knows these are the white man's colours. She takes off her shoes and walks about bare-foot, which gives her a festive feeling. Then she looks up at the clouds as she does every day and sees that the great spectacle is continuing up above. The gigantic crocodile with its single evil eye still guards the heavens and no longer moves. His eye resembles the eye of the white man when he flies into a rage. The crocodile does not change and remains fixed to the same spot. She goes down to the street to get something for her lunch, and purchases a large slice of tuna. "It is forbidden to eat meat today." She hangs the fish on the nail in the kitchen where the towel usually hangs, for this slice of fish clearly resembles a menacing face, one that will protect her. She is expecting the young psychiatrist Dr. Rabain, whom she knows from St. Anne's and who wants her to record her writings on mental illness on a Magnetophone. On this day the manuscript will be her most precious possession. She imagines that Rabain will ask her questions, and she will answer — a thorough cross-questioning — and that one day the recording will be broadcast throughout world on the radio. Both Rabain and the white man had encouraged her to complete her text.

The white man (Henri Michaux) is, as noted earlier, the exact image of her childhood vision of the Man of Jasmine. In the afternoon she asks her friend to phone a doctor she knows well. She realises that she has entered a new crisis. The doctor is not there, but they promise that he will visit her at seven in the evening.

That afternoon she begins setting the kitchen table for three guests: for the white man, Christian (his son),[56] and a Hungarian actor whom she had loved when she was twelve. Her anticipation of these guests also has religious connotations for her: of Good Friday and Christ's crucifixion. Christian seems to turn into Christ and the white man into God, but this is not linked to any sort of religious ecstasy. She allots these roles as if to two actors. She steps onto the veranda and puts out a large piece of cake for the birds. She knows that tomorrow the whole room will be full of birds, and that she will become Saint Francis of Assisi, and understand their language. She goes to her bedroom for half an hour, closing the door behind her. She lies down on her bed. In the twinkling of an eye the room becomes one of those at St. Anne's. Voices rise up from the garden surrounding the large building. The whole place has become a psychiatric clinic. The voices are those of the doctors and patients. She is certain that if she leaves her room, her friend, suddenly taken "very ill", would lie down in his bed and a rather masculine-looking woman-friend of hers would lie down in the one next to it. Both have been afflicted by an incredible transformation. Under the observation of the psychiatrists and nurses, and with the help of injections, the man will turn slowly into a woman and the woman into a man. They will copulate, feel themselves saved, and marry. As she leaves her bedroom she sees her friend, who has gone out onto the veranda. He does not cast even a single glance at the sky. He does not see the mighty crocodile. He does not see the images of the past rolling by in the clouds. He does not see the pure forms of the Baroque era, even though he is very fond of the Baroque. So he does not number among the initiates and the elect.

She feels a certain disdain for him, and begins to insult and disparage him. She blames her behaviour on a nervous attack. She throws a heavy ashtray at the glass door to the veranda. This action resembles a scene at her Parisian friends' flat, when she had thrown a glass at the wall and a cup at the floor. Shortly afterwards she leaves the flat without her keys or money. She has forgotten that she should wait for the doctor, her patience has vanished.

The evening is warm and pleasant. She walks to the Place de la Nation and takes a taxi. She asks to be taken to the Place de la Contrescarpe. She realises that she has no money for the fare, and so she gives the taxi driver a packet of Dutch cigarettes that she finds in her handbag as payment. The taxi driver growls: "Who wants to smoke this muck," but contents himself with that.

Dusk has arrived. She sees a number of youngsters on the Place de la Contrescarpe and in the rue Mouffetard. "They're waiting for you!" It is like a game. It is forbidden to speak with or look at one another.

All these young people, including Christian, somewhere or other, recognise and admire her. The atmosphere is once again festive.

She walks slowly down this street, the one she loves most in the whole of Paris. She enters number 88, the double, vertical infinity of the Hotel de l'Esperance where she had begun her life in Paris. The building exerts an irresistible attraction on her. She asks after the proprietor, M. Gustave, but he is away on his travels. She asks if they have a room for her, but, as ever, the hotel is fully booked. She orders a mint tea and drinks it without stopping to think that she cannot pay. She shakes hands with M. Mohamed and greets other North Africans whom she has been friends with for years. She leaves the hotel and walks down the street to the Place St. Médare. She is tired and looks for a bench to sit on, but the little park is closed. She carries on towards the mosque. She grows increasingly tired and, passing a café, sits down at a table. She sees pretty young girls in summer frocks out walking with their handbags. She is certain that these girls have been "despatched" to watch over her wherever she goes. At the same time she has the impression that she is in Hamburg on a street in St. Pauli, and that the girls are young prostitutes. She leaves her handbag with her cigarettes and French identity card on the table of the café as a sign that she has discovered a "fifth column of friends".

This also means liberation from her final burdens. She no longer has to carry anything. She counts the things she is wearing: 1) a coat, 2) a skirt, 3) a blouse, 4) a pair of underpants, 5) a brassiere, 6) a left shoe, 7) a right shoe and… 8)… herself.

Eight things which henceforth move with her through the world. She is under the sign of the perpendicular eternity.

She has entered a noble state.

She continues on her way to the mosque. The mosque's garden is open this evening. A large number of people are sitting there, enjoying the peaceful relaxation that it radiates, which is unique in all of Paris.

Immediately on entering the garden she asks the attendant to phone the psychiatrist Dr. Ferdiére, telling him that he will find the doctor's name in the telephone book under the address she gives him. The man jots down the doctor's name on a piece of paper. She asks him to tell the doctor: "Unica is waiting for you at the mosque."

She is convinced that he will phone Ferdiére, and so she sits and waits for him in garden.

She orders a mint tea which she avoids drinking because she hasn't the money to pay for it. She stays there for half an hour, waiting in vain for the doctor. Disappointed, she leaves the mosque, walks across the street, stops a passing car with a black driver and asks him if he knows where she can find a doctor nearby. She is at the end of her wits and has no idea how to continue without help. The driver motions, almost silently, to a nearby house, as if she might find a doctor there.

She stops beside a red traffic light which suddenly seems to have the properties of a telephone. She moves her hand in empty space, performing the necessary movements "on the dial" (which is invisible) to call the number 999. She "hears" a buzzing that arouses her expectations. She says "Hello, Christian, this is mummy, please come and fetch me at once."

She waits in vain for five minutes. The telephone remains silent. Her son does not answer. Feeling dejected and abandoned, she remains beside the telephone until an unfamiliar young man steps up to her. An emissary from the fifth column, she is sure of it now. Her saviour. She asks him whether he is *also sick* in order to strike up a conversation. "We're *all* sick," he answers calmly.

She starts to shiver and asks him to accompany her for a hot drink. He takes her to a nearby café and she orders tea. They sit in a corner. The proprietress is in the process of clearing up, they are the last customers.

She sits quite resolutely in her corner by the table, as if she wanted to remain there for the next couple of hours. She begins her vigil once more, waiting for the white man, his son Christian, the book dealer Flinker — an older friend of her son's whom she had picked to be one of his teachers, and to introduce him to art and literature. (Incidentally, it was Flinker whom she had seen disguised as a steward on the airplane from Paris to Frankfurt.)

She expects Doctor Ferdiére and Doctor Rabain, who will come with a Magnetophone to record her reading her text on mental illness.

But no one comes. Filled with pain and disappointment, she knocks her teacup from the table onto the floor.

She gets up and leaves without a word. She turns back and finds the house the black driver had indicated. She goes in and sees a young girl standing next to the lift. She asks her for the doctor. The girl doesn't know of any doctor in the building. So she sits on the stairs and decides to remain there until someone takes her to St. Anne's. A young couple descend the stairs. She asks them for a cigarette. Neither the man nor the woman have cigarettes on them. Then she tells them that she feels ill and is no longer able to walk, and that they should fetch a police car to take her to St. Anne's.

Ten minutes later the two youngsters take her out to the street and a large police car draws up, and, getting in, she asks the policemen to take her straight to St. Anne's. The policemen are friendly, but avoid talking with her.

The journey begins. A journey that seems very long to her. She tries to look out through the barred windows. She has the impression that the car trip has something festive about it, as if the artists who live in the sixth arrondissement have gathered outside and are waiting for her. Finally the car stops and she is asked to get out. She enters a very large room in which a number of policemen are sitting. She finds a secluded place in the corner and sits down opposite a typewriter.

A policeman comes over to her table in order to use the machine. She immerses herself in her thoughts and does not take anything else in. After a while she looks up and sees a number of policemen opposite her, staring in her direction. She studies them with curiosity and sees that they are fat, motionless, and as white as corpses, and that their faces are stamped by an extraordinary, bestial and obscene malevolence. Suddenly she realises that these are not real French policemen, but SS men and top Nazi officials who have been kept imprisoned, unable to escape, in the deep, dark cellars of the Paris police prefecture and who tonight have been given one unique "chance" to walk along the streets in the fresh air, disguised as gendarmes, while closely guarded by real ones. Afterwards they will be led back to their subterranean vaults, then one day will be killed once and for all.

She feels the need to smoke, gets up and hesitantly approaches two desks located behind a barrier. Sitting behind one of the desks is an astonishing person in police uniform: him! His hair is reddish blond, his eyes blue. He is busy writing. He looks as if he is wearing make-up. He has disguised himself as a policeman. She is amused by this comedy. He is here to protect her. He does not leave her, but it is forbidden for them to look at one another and talk. Nevertheless, she asks him politely whether he can give her a cigarette.

He does not reply and does not look her way. She remembers what Max Ernst once said to her while they were discussing him: "He is an actor."

And how she had added: "I read in one of his books that he no longer looks in the mirror, although obviously he has to look in the mirror every morning when he shaves."

She returns to her seat opposite the typewriter. She watches as the policemen make coffee and place cups on a table. She sees a box of sugar cubes, gets up and takes one in order to overcome her desire to smoke. A policeman sees her and wags his finger at her in fun, shaking his head in remonstration. Then someone arrives and ushers her somewhere else. She is not quite sure how she has suddenly come to be in this small white room with its white covered bed. A man and woman in white coats. Doctors? She asks the doctor for a cigarette and is given one. A second person in white enters, a man who instils fear in her. He is identical to an apparition she had seen in the clouds on 6.6.66: the white, tangible soul of a Jew whom the Nazis had gassed in a concentration camp. He has blond curls. His curls form two horns which have nothing to do with the Devil, but rather look like two small flames, just like Moses in the illustrated children's Bible she had owned many years ago. Moses, who on some occasion she can no longer recall had flames on his head. She is scared by this re-incarnated Jewish soul. He smiles. She is relieved when he leaves the room. His smile was sinister, as if he wanted to torture her right here on this bed because she comes from the race that set up the concentration camps.

As if a sluice had been opened, she pours out her confessions to the doctor. Disclosures which no one but a real doctor, who is pledged to silence, may hear.

She tells of her tragic meeting with the white man. He listens to her with a white, attentive and motionless face.

She discloses his name. Later she can no longer recall who had taken her back to her cell. She has the impression that she had passed through the hands of another pair of figures in white, a man and a woman who seemed to be mentally ill. They tell her to undress so that she can hand over her brassière. She recalls that prisoners have to hand over their shoe laces, belts and ties before being locked in their cells so that they will not hang themselves.

Then the door is locked behind her. She is alone. A blue night-light glows from the ceiling of her cell. She takes off her skirt and blouse and lies down on the clean white bed.

It is impossible for her to sleep. She begins a never-ending song. She has the feeling that her voice is very beautiful. She sings in French for the first time in her life. The text rhymes effortlessly to form simple and childlike verses. She is amazed that her command of the language is so good that she is able to sing these poems, which she makes up on the spur of the moment. The song alternates between two different melodies:

1. The old melody of a poor, abandoned orphan that she heard the young girl in Wittenau sing one night, and which she and Hans Bellmer had made "their" song; and

2. The tune of the famous French lullaby: *"Fais dodo…"*

The words of this poem, which she makes up as she goes along and instantly forgets, revolve around the two psychiatrists, Doctor Ferdiére and Doctor Rabain. The poem is full of affection for the two doctors, a small anthem of adoration. During the pauses in her song she hears a group of listeners applauding just outside her cell and laughing in a charming way, and knows that Ferdiére, Rabain and Michaux are among them. She adds an extra verse for the latter. It seems to her that she keeps singing for hours on end, and the applause and quiet laughter is repeated whenever she takes a break. No, she has not been abandoned, people are taking care of her, just as they had promised they would. She should not feel afraid.

For a moment it seems to her that the two patients who had dressed up as doctors have entered her room, turned her onto her stomach, pulled down the blanket that covered her, and given her an injection. But since she cannot find a needle mark, she interprets these events as follows: they are two patients who are already on the road to recovery. The real doctors have given them the opportunity to do something useful: they are being allowed to perform the role of doctors so that perhaps one day, when they have recovered, they can become actual doctors, because as former mental patients they will understand their patients far better because they will have personally experienced their illnesses. They touch her with a finger to simulate the needle of the syringe.

She falls asleep and next morning is woken by a nurse who hands her a towel and a cake of soap through the opening in the cell door. She is told to wash herself. A thin trickle of water runs from a tap into a small basin. Shortly afterwards the water is turned off from outside the cell so that the patient won't do anything silly with the tap. She is given bread and coffee. She drinks eagerly, but does not eat anything. After several hours spent stretched out on her bed, she is taken to the doctor.

It is not clear to her whether she is being examined by a doctor or a plain-clothes policeman. On her way to the doctor's room she is led across the same elastic rubber floor she had encountered in St. Anne's, and suddenly she is convinced that she is in the same hospital. Later she is unable to recall the questions the doctor (or policeman) put to her, nor her replies. But she gives him her address and tells them that she left her handbag in a café near the mosque. He asks her if she would like them to tell Bellmer where she is, and she says yes. As she is brought back to her cell, she walks once again over the elastic rubber flooring, which continues to fascinate her. At that moment she sees two policemen bringing in a man. Each of the policemen is holding him firmly by one arm. The man's face is completely insane. The policemen let him go and he runs like a wild thing until he reaches the rubber floor, where he sinks slightly when he stands on it. But he does not jump about on it the way she had done at St. Anne's. He looks all around with a very agitated expression. The cell door closes behind her, and she lies back down on her bed. She begins to study the door closely and attentively. The brown paint is damaged at the bottom and around the opening. The cell's many occupants have kicked the bottom of the door to show that they want to be brought back to liberty. The bottom and sides of the door likewise show the traces of the multitude of fists that have hammered at it over the years, crying out for someone to help them in their loneliness.

She begins to read figures in this damaged paintwork. She can clearly detect the tall figure of the white man approaching her along a straight road lined on both sides by trees. Some distance behind, she sees herself walking along the street towards him. She sees him again at a different spot on the door, now turning his back on her and walking off.

She spends a long time staring at these images, which start to move under her weary gaze. She sees herself quite distinctly, walking towards the white man: the distance between them diminishes, but they get no closer to one another. A certain distance always remains between them.

She feels an extraordinary attraction to this door and wonders how she could acquire it and take it home with her. She realises that this is impossible, which is sad.

Unsettled by the moving figures on the door, she averts her gaze and looks at the wall by her side, which is painted in thick strokes of bright blue gloss to give it a slightly raised pattern.

She looks at this paintwork and discovers faces, just as she had done as a child or when ill with fever. A mass of faces huddled together. Each face looks different, yet they all seem to belong to one enormous family. Their features are all related.

Their features are mobile, their mouths twist into a grin, they roll their eyes — they are just as capable of transforming into sweet smiles as into grimaces of rage, misery or madness.

She looks away and casts her eyes to the floor, wherever she looks she sees moving faces. She had once said: "I am obsessed by faces when I draw." A few hours pass while she is completely absorbed in watching this spectacle. Among these faces, which sometimes are surrounded by exquisitely drawn petals and leaves, she recognises some like those she has drawn herself: from Red Indian, Oriental or Asian peoples. Then she suddenly discovers animals among the faces and plants, animals that she had also attempted to draw: birds, fish and insects. She even sees the most fantastic *combinations* of animals and humans merged together in impossible but completely harmonious ways. She sees *new* creatures that she had never thought of before. This spectacle is an invaluable drawing lesson for her, but to her great regret she has to admit that she will never be able to render such beautiful and fantastic creatures with the necessary technical perfection.

She resolves never to leave this cell again. It is impossible to feel bored here. She watches a fascinating, never-ending film, and realises she can learn a thing or two for her drawings. She has a bed here. That is the most important thing, because she loves to lie in bed and dream.

She looks around and notes that there is enough room in the cell for her gramophone, her records and a table to work on. The main thing now is to get permission to install a table and chair in her cell. She starts to decorate the room very nicely in her thoughts. She gets fed. She is all on her own. She can do whatever she wants here.

She must ask them to bring her some paper, pens and black Chinese ink, and above all her gramophone, she has an urgent need to listen to very powerful, loud and deafening music. (There have been times in her life when her craving for music has been as strong as an addict's for drugs.)

She is full of confidence. Someone or other will come and bring it all, everything she needs. She decides never to leave this cell. She wants to remain here until she breathes her last. She needs only to look at one place on the door to see the two of them walking slowly towards one another, and at another they are walking side-by-side, slowly through a sunlit field. She is completely saved and happy.

She will attempt drawings as fine as the pictures she sees in the walls and the floor. Satisfied, she gets up and looks out of the opening in the cell door into the corridor, which is empty. She looks in the other direction and sees another cell door with an opening. It appears to be very dark in this cell. She has the feeling that this cell is a damp, black vault without any light, and that some insane Gretchen, driven mad by her love for Doctor Heinrich Faust, is lying inside this dungeon on a filthy bed of straw.

Then a pale face with long, black uncombed hair appears in the opening — a girl with large, black eyes. She extends her hand through the opening, holding out an empty plastic bowl. She calls out: *"Madame, s'il vous plaît, — à boire s'il vous plaît!"*[57]

But no one comes.

She, for her part, hopes that a nurse will appear so she can ask her for a cigarette. They call out in unison: *"Madame, s'il vous plaît."* She sees a table in the corridor. On the table there is a box of matches. The sight of the matchbox awakens an almost unbearable desire in her to smoke.

They shout in vain. Resigned, she goes back to her bed. All of a sudden her door is unlocked and Doctor Rabain appears in the company of a nurse. He has brought her a large bouquet of red roses. The nurse fetches a vase of water, arranges the roses in a vase and places it on the floor. It is incredible just how beautiful the roses look in this ugly cell. Doctor Rabain takes a look round the cell and says: "It's simply ghastly here."

She asks him for a cigarette, and he gives her a full packet of Gauloises. In that moment her courage rises in a steep, optimistic curve. In this moment she is truly saved. The cigarette is lit by the nurse. She is not allowed to have matches in her cell. So she is compelled to light each cigarette from the one before.

Doctor Rabain tells her that he had discovered late yesterday evening that she had been brought to the infirmary. He had looked through the opening in her door and seen that she was asleep.

He has also brought her a colourful picture postcard from her daughter, which she asks him to read to her. They both laugh at the funny way he pronounces German.

He tells her that she must go to St. Anne's for two days, and from there she will be taken to the Maison-Blanche sanatorium in Neuilly-sur-Marne.

He promises to visit her there. She props the postcard against the vase of flowers and feels even more at home in her cell. During her first internment in St. Anne's, Rabain had been the first doctor to whom she could open up her heart with complete trust. Since then he has become a good friend.

He it was who had encouraged her to finish her text. The white man, the first person to whom she had mentioned it, had been ready to provide her with money for upkeep until she finished it. It was unbelievably friendly and generous of him. But she had been forced to interrupt her work when she was interned in St. Anne's.

She spends the second night in her cell and falls asleep without singing.

The next day she is fetched from her cell. She leaves the roses for her successor and is driven to St. Anne's, where she is given a nightgown and told to lie down in bed.

Her clothes and shoes are placed in the custody of a nurse. She is in a very large, brightly lit dormitory. All the beds seem to be occupied. A number of patients are wearing strait-jackets, and are tied by their arms and legs to their beds. In the bed next to her is an older woman in delirium. She watches this woman with great curiosity, because she seems to be completely unaware of her surroundings. But she has to study the woman for some time before she can understand her imaginings and inner state.

This woman is in the midst of an extremely intense erotic crisis. Her hands are tied, her arms not visible. She throws back her head and pokes out a wriggling tongue. Her body arches upwards like a bridge. With enormous effort she attempts to get close to her imaginary partner. It is clear to see that she is in the throes of intense sensual pleasure. She moans and whispers incomprehensible words. Her face twists into a grimace. Finally she slumps down on her mattress and rests, trembling. After not even five minutes the scene repeats. Without a male partner and without touching herself, she experiences physical rapture more than thirty times in one hour.

Sometimes she opens her eyes briefly and awakens from her delirium for a few minutes. In the short moments when she is aware of her surroundings she punishes herself, slapping herself with her hands (which the nurse has untied).

She lashes at her face with both hands. Then folds them and mutters prayers with her lips. She crosses herself repeatedly. It is simultaneously fascinating and embarrassing to watch her.

The sight of all this makes her feel ashamed to be a woman.

This woman has an aura about her of complete license and obsession! And is neither young nor attractive. She has no teeth. She is pure obscenity. She is skinny and she sweats. She never ceases yielding to her imaginary partner, but even a spectacle like this becomes boring when constantly repeated.

In this posture (the moment of rapture) the woman resembles one of those astonishing cephalopods that Bellmer has often drawn: women consisting of just a head and abdomen, their arms replaced by legs. In other words, she has no arms. She even has the protruding tongue of Bellmer's drawings of cephalopods; there is something outrageous about it.

Finally the woman quietens down, thoroughly exhausted. She falls asleep. A young man appears beside her bed and sits down at her side. He kisses and strokes her. He says: "Don't be afraid mummy, we shan't desert you." She opens her eyes for a moment, but does not recognise her son. He remains by her side for half an hour and watches while his mother sleeps. Then he leaves without a word.

It is very quiet in the dormitory. Opposite her is an old woman who is bound by her hands and feet. She thrashes her head from side to side on the pillows. She has a large growth on her head.

She is tempted to think that the woman also has a growth inside her head, a brain tumour that has driven her insane.

She gets up and asks for a cigarette from a nurse who smokes. She receives one along with a light. She returns to her bed and smokes. She feels at home in St. Anne's. She doesn't worry about a thing. She has reached the end of her journey.

But she wants to see a doctor. This desire becomes so strong that she gets up again and walks to the table where the nurses are drinking their coffee. She pounds her fist on the table and shouts: "When you're brought here to St. Anne's as a patient you've the right to see a doctor at once!"

No one replies. Offended, she returns to her bed. Five minutes later a nurse comes and injects her with a sedative.

An hour later she is asleep. But before falling asleep she hears, from the upper storeys of St. Anne's, the voice of her man-like friend, screaming a loud, anxious, "No!" She knows what that means. This friend has also gone mad and been brought to St. Anne's where they will give her injections so as to slowly transform her into a man under the observation of the psychiatrists. This "No!" is a scream of protest at this transformation. She suspects that Bellmer has also been brought to St. Anne's, so as to be given a course of treatment to turn him into a woman.

Such transformations into the opposite sex seem to entail certain dangers.

She wakes shortly before six o'clock as preparations are being made for the patients' supper. The patients have tables on castors beside their beds and eat their meals lying down. After supper she is given another cigarette and at her request, Binoctal, to send her to sleep.

She enjoys lying in bed and being waited on. Since childhood her bed has been the place in which she feels safest in this uncanny and dubious world. The bed, in which she can write and draw and dream, is her last refuge from life; indeed, for weeks and months on end her bed is the only place where she can carry on living, during the long periods of hopeless, apathetic depression that arrive with such ruthless regularity after her periods of madness and delightful hallucinations. In this state she remains lying in bed with her eyes closed for hours on end and manages to avoid all thought. During one such unbearable depression, she spent so long in bed that her skin became sore and the nurse had physically to force her to get up, walk about and occupy herself in a normal way.

She falls asleep, waking several hours later and remaining awake until morning. The woman next to her is fast asleep. She looks at the others: one single person, tied up in a strait-jacket, is jabbering incomprehensible words in a husky, utterly distorted voice. Until dawn breaks, when at last her voice, scarcely human, falls silent.

She is glad when breakfast is served. She is hungry and thirsty. A good sign. The patients are untied and proceed to an ugly room where they wash and comb themselves. There are no towels, toothbrushes or combs for the patients who have been brought in by the police and haven't anything on their person. Not even a flannel. In such cases, patients are given a dampened nightgown to wash with. They dry themselves on the same nightgown. There are a couple of combs in a tin box — and there is also a mirror. After breakfast she asks the nurse who constantly smokes for another cigarette, which she is given with a light. Ashtrays are available. She walks around the dormitory. She feels fine. She studies the others.

At around ten in the morning she is taken to a doctor. For this she is given a pretty dark blue bathrobe. Later she is unable to recall what she says to the doctor. But at any rate she does not make any uncontrolled disclosures like she had to the young doctor on the night she was taken to the police station, when she had revealed the secret of a name. In any case, this conversation with the doctor is very brief and probably unimportant. She tells him that she left her handbag on a café table in the 5th arrondissement, near the mosque, and asks if someone would look for it. He reassures her, and she returns to her bed. She gets up and walks around the large dormitory once more. She tries to count the patients: there are roughly 28 to 30 of them. She sees a motionless figure lying in bed, her head bandaged in gauze and cotton wool. A grey face with closed eyes. A nurse is standing next to the bed, taking the injured woman's pulse. She thinks: this patient has leapt out of the window and probably has a dangerous skull fracture. Suddenly the nurse rushes out and shortly after returns with a young doctor, who also takes the bandaged woman's pulse. At this moment she dies. The nurses, perhaps five in all, come to the dead woman's bed and with a sad expression shake the doctor by the hand. Perhaps he had attempted to save her with an operation. He is probably a surgeon, for there is a surgical ward at St. Anne's.

The doctor leaves and the nurses push the woman's bed away from the others. A nurse arrives with a large disinfection sprayer (?) and douses the dead woman and the bed with a liquid (?). Then the whole bed is wheeled out.

She carries on walking about the dormitory and wants to smoke. She comes to the bed of a Chinese (?) patient. This woman has an astonishing, mask-like face, and sings in a foreign language. She is familiar enough with the sound of Asiatic languages to recognise she is Asian. Ah, now she *understands*: the woman comes from Vietnam and had wanted to immolate herself on the streets of Paris in protest at the Vietnam War, at the American bombing campaign. The police had prevented her from carrying out this suicidal protest and brought her to St. Anne's as a mental patient. She scrutinises the somewhat wild face of the Vietnamese and listens to her revolutionary singing. At the same time she arrives at an explanation for the self-immolations in Vietnam (in Saigon) that she had read about in the papers: the suicides (priests and women) had been injected with an anaesthetic so they would not feel any pain when they burned. She asks the Vietnamese for a cigarette, for she sees that she has a packet of Gauloises on her table. The Asiatic at once hides the packet in her hand and cries: "*Non!*"

This arouses in her enormous contempt for this woman and simultaneously, for the first time in her life, contempt for the Asian race, which she has loved and respected since childhood as a result of their artworks, which she had come to admire at an early age in her parent's house, and also because she prefers the form of the Asian face to any other. She hates this woman from the bottom of her heart, a woman who has not grasped that mad women who are locked away in a psychiatric clinic must help one another.

Smoking is her only drug, and she has consumed cigarettes ever since her eighteenth year. Smoking is as important to her as sleep. At times of fearful poverty in Berlin she would spend her last money on cigarettes rather than on bread. Better to go hungry, but smoke. Smoking instantly gives her the pleasing feeling of luxury.

As for drugs, she only knows the effects of Pervatin, which enables one to write without stop for a day and a night. She has smoked hashish without feeling the slightest effect, except perhaps as a stimulant for her work.

In her mind smoking also has something to do with love, although she finds it difficult to define this exactly. An unhappy love! She inhales the smoke deep into her lungs. She has a longing to be filled, to be permeated, and has inhaled and exhaled for year and years without quenching this thirst. It is a miracle that smoke doesn't pour out from every opening of her body. As for love, she also finds it in the sea, which embraces one completely, which gives support and the feeling of floating.

After two days she is driven with other patients to Maison-Blanche in Neuilly-sur-Marne. She is quickly taken to see a young doctor, and she tells him that she makes drawings. He immediately gives her white drawing paper, nibs and a pot of black Chinese ink. The struggle to get hold of cigarettes recommences. The nurses give her one now and again, but far too few to prevent her from becoming more nervous than she already is. The first to visit her are George Visat and his wife Suzanne. They bring her cigarettes, chocolates, and a number of copper plates with two engraving needles, and motivate her to work. There could be no better present here than the possibility of work. She begins and completes a series of engravings that are intended for a book containing a number of her anagram poems, which George Visat will publish under the title *Oracles and Spectacles*. The friendship with Georges and Suzanne, who come and visit her at Maison-Blanche (a psychiatric clinic) every visiting-day, is of inestimable value to her, because, although she is surrounded by lots of people, she always feels lonely. There are roughly sixty sick women and girls in this building, many of whom will never leave the clinic. She becomes friendly with 18 year-old Micheline, who has been here for three years and with whom she goes for walks every day through the beautiful, large park to shop for the other patients at the tobacconist's, the newsagent's, and the canteen. The patients are obliged to work at this clinic, too, for several hours in the morning and the afternoon: embroidering and knitting. She, however, is excused from this, because she is concentrating on her engravings in the refectory.

After her initial interview with a young psychiatrist, the staff decide which sedatives she must gulp down: Haloperidol, Keithon and Nozinan. These medications cause her hallucinations, or are they caused by her morbid state? When she is lying on her bed she fixes her gaze on the glass-fibre doors of the wardrobe and sees a myriad of faces, animals and landscapes which are constantly moving and changing their expressions, as in a never-ending film. These hallucinations, not dissimilar to her interpretations of the patterns in those doors, unsettle her as much as they enchant her. Gradually, though, it becomes a torture for her, goes into the garden to escape these wardrobe doors and sit on a bench in the sun, she is tempted to see fantastic, moving creatures in the grass or the simple meadow blossoms. She cannot tolerate this condition any longer and asks the doctor to give her more Nozinan, a medication to which she has grown accustomed over the years.

The doctors fill her with insurmountable distrust. She asks the young psychiatrist whether he is a *real* psychiatrist, and he answers with a slight smile: "Yes, I think so."

She comes to believe that the female doctor and her assistant are sick, two mad women who have simply disguised themselves as doctors with the consent of the real psychiatrists, so as to give them the chance of doing something "useful".

Likewise she is convinced that some of the nurses are in reality, sick, and may at any moment carry out something quite appalling and unimaginable on her body.

She also imagines that unheard-of obscenities are taking place between the patients and the nurses in this institution. In addition she suspects that the psychiatrists have established a "central thought agency" — she remembers this expression from a utopian novel by Franz Werfel: *The Star of the Unborn*,[58] — and this thought agency focuses the suggestive willpower of a number of the doctors. Five or six doctors will concentrate together, for instance, on the abdomen of one of the patients and put her in a state of sensual rapture. They take devilish delight in repeating this several times a day and making the patient even crazier than she already is. During periods of normality she asks herself in all seriousness whether psychiatrists have ever sexually abused their mad patients in the clinic.

In this connection, she recalls the words she heard on some occasion or other: one cannot think of anything that will not come to be true in some form or another.

When she watches television she has the impression that the newscaster can see her, just as she sees him, and is speaking just for her. She feels allied to him. He belongs to the fifth column. The very moment she gets toothache, say, and is thinking of going to the dentist's, she hears the newscaster say: "*C'est ta faute.*"[59] — meaning: why didn't you come to me earlier. The radio broadcaster's voice is that of her dentist, who knows that at that very moment she is suffering from toothache.

She sheds bitter tears when she learns from the television of the death of a highly acclaimed German cartoon film-maker (Kaskeline), whom she had admired as a girl while working at the Ufa film studios.[60] She sees marionettes whose features resemble those of the film-maker's wife. These marionettes are his children which, so she now believes, had been burned like their Jewish father in a Nazi concentration camp. Kaskeline had once made a puppet film at Ufa.

She becomes convinced that Kaskeline and his children died a terrible death under the Nazis, and forgets that she had seen him, full of life and charming, in a bus in Berlin after the war.

She is taken to a psychologist who conducts various tests on her: interpreting various blots, answering countless questions printed on small cards, and interpreting reproductions of paintings and drawings by inventing little stories about them. As if hypnotised, she stares at the small scar at the root of the psychologist's nose: the scar turns into a tiny face which makes distinct, ever-changing grimaces.

She mentions this apparition and complains of it to him and the psychiatrists confirm that she is suffering from visual disturbances.

She spends two pleasant summer months at Maison-Blanche.

Bellmer visits her, together with the art dealer André-François Petit. The Visats continue visiting her, bringing cigarettes and chocolates; she is not alone.

Her last crisis is not severe and she is soon over it. Only when she no longer feels any desire for hallucinations, for the beautiful apparitions which her mental illness is able to bestow on her, will she be ready to become healthy. Through her illness she has become acquainted with a number of helpful and useful psychiatrists, to whom she remains highly indebted — apart from one.

This one doctor made her realise what a man like Antonin Artaud had been forced to put up with.

THE WHITENESS
WITH THE RED SPOT

ABANDONED TO CHANCE OR:
THE SUM OF THE FACES AWAITS ITS RESULT[61]

•

ERMENONVILLE, FEBRUARY '59

PART I

Dedicated to my son
Christian and to the
9 times table

My eyes have become long-sighted:
they see distant objects clearly. I notice this
because it used to be different.
Might that have something to do with my favourite pastime —
finding ANAGRAMS? —

Nowadays when the object of my longings and privations approaches, when he
is suddenly present, I tend to be embarrassed, wish he would go away, may the
Devil take him — but at any rate
back to the place where until that day
my longing had tried so gently to explore it.
And that is my inner contradiction — my disbelief.

My heart seems to stop with joy…
but then the inevitable comes, my
embarrassment What am I to make of my fortune
when I have made myself so at home
with my misfortune?
At the same time I wish myself dead — to die
together with my fortune.
And that is my egotism.

Anyone who has ever made a kite

with a child — and who has allowed themselves
to be guided more by the child than by
the actual instructions for constructing a kite,
knows how many smiling gazes of pure joy
are exchanged while making it.
And that is the best part of building a kite with a child.

What follows then — that the kite won't fly,
or only *half* flies, crashes to the ground, is
torn or forgotten or even though it is new,
gets left with the other junk on top of a cupboard —
is of no importance compared with the unalloyed pleasure of making a kite with
a child.
And just as it is with the kite, so it is with other things.

As our tragedy assumed its unbending form, you
saw with other eyes. You looked away when
you answered me: "A knife is better than
a friend." (I had asked you whether you had at last
found a friend.)

●

Just when the signs which were to describe the end of my
childhood already in place, I had a
dream:
resting beside a heap of glowing coals
on an icy winter street that leads to the left,
always to the left, is a black patch — in the midst of the whiteness.
It is a grimy dwarf, as I discover on approaching.
His keen rolling black eyes
follow my trembling anxiety as I have to
pass him by.

Later this dream is interpreted to me as my fear
of men.
Thanks to my fear of that science which bears the
name of psychology (analysis), I have not yet investigated
the scientific interpretation of dreams.
My *own* interpretation is more plausible to me:
it would seem to me that the ugly dwarf
is my own life:
crippled, when I would have loved it to have been beautiful,
fixed to the ground when I would loved to have danced,
floated and flown.

Hostile, with murderous intentions, while
I would have loved to have felt trust; trust, so
that I could open myself up, flow, drink from the stream
and drown therein…

But quite to the contrary and against all
expectations, the first female eyes
that I saw at the beginning of my life
instilled in me an unconquerable fear of spiders.
And later things were not much better.

Thus I divided myself very early on into two halves.
(There are a considerable number of images
for this familiar process, all different yet all with
the same meaning. I have chosen *the* image that
first occurred to me.)
The one half lacked the power to resistance and self-defence, and,
despised by the other for its
inexperience and tendency to stumble.
received a regular dressing down. The other half,

however, looked on, shook its head
and repeated the adults' cruel remarks:
"That's what comes of it! Didn't I tell
you so? Just carry on like that and
see what happens!"
And this division torments me
to this day.

•

Human trickery with their eyes! Whereas one might think
that nothing could be more honest than their eyes...
But sometimes one doesn't know
which way to look.
Slit or sewn up, these lids are able to open up into
a large and oh so encompassing tiger-gaze.
What use is that to them? At once they shrivel up again,
disappear, as if the unheard scream had been only
a pitiful whimper.
And those gestures — those gestures remind me
of the sad masses of cheap black winter coats which
hang like peas in a pod in long rows
in off-the-peg clothes stores.
And this litany has bolted me shut.
What had I expected? (For I know that I am
right to wait.) What have I hoped for
with such madness?
And this madness is my one strength.

So now it has arrived, together with the bleak summer days
of this miserable climate in which I live.
My situation has changed. It distinguishes itself
now by the delights of pure sadness.

A most dignified situation.

The situation has arrived. It has explained itself and
no longer stirs itself. I have acquired a counterpart!
And that is the proof.
And that is my source of pride, my stubborn defiance
of my circumstances until now.

I have always lived solely in the hope of
acquiring a counterpart. As I said at the
outset — and can only repeat it here —
it makes me embarrassed, as embarrassed
as profusion suddenly embarrasses.
And hence my preference for distance.

My childish feelings come back to life,
aided by the move from Paris to the foggy landscape
of Ermenonville. I see trees. I hear the birds.
What a restorative: sky, birds, clouds.
What a help to me, after having turned about
so earnestly, to walk, if possible,
in his little footsteps from earlier,
or at least to act as if…

Trees, bushes, the open skies, yes even
the fog helps.
And yet another miracle, a second one: I no longer
regret that I didn't throw myself out of the window
at the age of twelve, as I had intended.
And that? Is that supposed to be hope?

End of Part I

à Christian *mon fils*
à H M Herman Melville

MANUSCRIT N^{O.} 3

PART II.

By giving up all hope of warmth, I murder the cold.

How good I would feel if I could be something
that called itself neither man nor woman. Perhaps I would
then come to myself — or to you?
As far as I can tell I have not received too much
from either man or woman, but enough
to feel it as an impediment.

My intermittent efforts to be neither the one
nor the other have not produced any
result. Why? Because I *alone* have taken
great pains to address this. So I never managed
to bring anything to a successful conclusion.
I have no one with whom I can discuss the matter.
In other words: no fellow sufferer. For only
he could give me the encouragement needed
to continue in my efforts.
And that is my quandary.

●

As if my son were already ripe in years
and approaching death, his eyes,
which search for mine just as I search for his,
intersect with the eyes of the one who is casting looks into

empty space. A notion that is still unclear,
far too new to be defined.
Nevertheless it crystallises, seeks a place
to reside in me and comes across as if it were true.
And we will see — see this
new calamity which is already
on its way…
You ghostly gaze! Shy and radiant,
wicked with loneliness and humour; your darkness,
seemingly without beginning
and thus without end, shines
through my dream-bright rooms. I ask myself
whether angels might have such eyes?

But this shy smile soon disappears,
the eternal youth of this singular smile
sinks like the long July day with no night,
the long, radiant day
that is never bestowed
on us.
And that is my despair.

•

The masculine character is as incomprehensible
to me as the female character. No
path leads that way, no
possibilities for me. I cannot
and will not ever get to like it there.
What terrible shame overcomes me when I discover the male or female
in myself!

I thought that the encounter with
a human being — and here I am
talking of the encounter with a
man — could make the curtains
vanish. More than this: that this event
would be the main outcome
of such an encounter.
And that is my belief and my delusion!

●

Meanwhile — I am getting old. I wrap myself
tighter in my velvet door curtain
which has grown dusty, and feel cold.
Hopeless — quite beyond hope!
But the dream becomes all the more dazzling!
Transparent! Brightness! — So bright!
And that is my consolation.

Early on, with an instinct that I quickly betrayed
— namely that it is DISTANCE,
and nothing but DISTANCE, that constitutes
for me the marvellous — as a child I dreamt
of a marriage with a white-haired, paralysed
man who educated me. I saw myself at his feet.
Teaching and listening, that was how
this marriage was, which took place
in a park beneath the eternal July sky.
And naturally he was handsome
and had a castle. I have not retained much of his image
apart from his paleness
(obviously related to his hair, his skin

and his eyes). His hands also. Behind us blossomed
the jasmine, immutable.
Nothing changed.
Apart from his large, precious but
frightful gaze, he also touched me
with his voice. I don't think
he shook hands with me.
This marriage was my supreme happiness.
I believe I have never wavered in this
conviction.
And that is the source of my discontent.
My great discontent with my
life and with its possibilities.
And that is the meaning of my tale of
a life spent together.

•

Whenever I have to appear before strangers
my official smile slips sideways and distorts my appearance.
Doubtless the result of training: one puts on a friendly
face when saying "good morning," and in this way
smiling little good-morning-sayers have been
propelled since time immemorial from monster to malediction.
For all that, I used to belong more to the
"ungrateful wretches," to the rebellious kind. *That* is the
only training that is really entrenched in me!
How much it takes to be the princess
on the pea…
But I prefer to relate this miracle in
Hans Christian Andersen's words:
"The old queen went to the bedroom,

removed all the bedding and put a pea
on the base of the bed; she then took
twenty mattresses and placed them on the pea,
and then twenty eiderdowns
on top of them.
The princess had to spend the night
in this bed.
The next day the old queen asked her
how she had slept.
"Oh, terribly," replied the princess,
"I hardly slept a wink the whole night long.
God knows what was in my bed.
I was lying on something hard,
and I am black and blue all over.
It's simply awful!"
So the old queen saw that she was a real
princess, for she had felt the pea
through twenty mattresses
and twenty eiderdowns.
Only a proper princess could have
such a fair skin. The prince then took her
as his wife, for now he knew that he had a
real princess, and the pea was placed in a
museum, where, if no one has stolen it,
it can be seen to this day.
Yes, that was a real story!"

And that is my shortcoming, that is my flaw.

•

After so many silly days of laughter,
this day was serious. Almost in tears…

Tears?... Yes, don't you realise
who is standing there before you?
Everything behind me shrivels
to a spot on the carpet in front of me:
two feet beside each other. Above — in all likelihood? —
a face, which I only later come to understand,
one feature at a time, from a distance.
No one smiles. Perhaps experiences
like this hinder smiles? Experiences
which follow the good days:

Up above, where mostly there are two faces,
people continue to smile, to laugh even, but most of all
they talk, while further down,
deeper, that is, the bones buckle
under the terrible attempt to
keep-holding-one's-ground.
Blue noonday sky in spring,
how often have you turned black, in a
flash, the same way the whirling dizziness
begins, that sudden dissolution of what one calls
certainty. At least *once* —
and it makes me shudder to think of it.
I have watched this blackening process
with appalling clarity, because
the person who has been annihilated
does not always look up at the sky.
The familiar panic starts and it has its good side,
it tortures one to the point of having to make a decision: flight!
In this way excess baggage is discarded.
Gradually one sneers at it all, doesn't give a damn

for one's homeland, although absurd hopes
often begin to blossom at the most inopportune moments.
O human monstrosity! Instead
of renouncing him at last, as ever I want all that
has been made for me. I would sooner doubt
my own existence.
At which point I descend into hell!
And that is my defence and my pride,
my curtain, the one half of me — hope
and hopelessness — almost everything…

As if from a mosaic image that was totally smashed long ago,
the years wash its fragments
onto my shore. Occasionally a larger piece.
So I had to gather them. Carefully fitting
one fragment to the next. Which produced the hint
of an image, infinitely slowly. What once
was fiery — eagerness, curiosity
and mad impetuousness — is now only laziness.
The idiotic pace of my life has made a donkey
of me. Any moment the bone-softening
elixir of inertia will flow into my limbs.
Those days when I still ran are past.
Heaven knows what I kept thinking I could see there…

Today, assuming it is not also an optical illusion,
the "image" approaches me while I pretend to be sitting without
any expectations in my wing chair.
And that is my malicious manner, my revenge!

So keep quiet now, completely quiet, hands open,
these useless hands which, even when

they are fully convinced that they have grasped
something, are unable to hold on to a thing.
I repeat: keep quiet, with open hands
while the image approaches.
In order to avenge myself!
To avenge myself for this and for that —
and for everything, almost everything…!
And that is my readiness to deceive, as well as
my readiness to be deceived.

I have such a revulsion for speed
that I shall hardly get to see the world.
So farewell: Ireland, India, China —
farewell, unvisited.

Once I received a visit, or was it twice?
From someone who knows everything. A singular
(or threefold) person. He gives me to understand
that his reason for coming is simply
to bestow the honour of his presence on me,
to introduce me to society, show me around…
He also intimated that, if I would but wish it
from the bottom of my heart, he could educate,
elevate, dismay, teach, elucidate, entrance me.
Even help me fly —
(Well — if *that's* true???)

Sadly he arrives on one of my weak days,
on a day, that is, when I am too healthy
(the brevity of my periods of health should have made me
suspicious.) Naturally another
of these fragments floats into my room

as he enters; I pick it up carefully
so as to piece it to the others.
(This business with these fragments
which keep turning up
has something devilish about it!)
And that is my failing!
I should never even have started assembling this collection.
And that is my weakness, my failing,
my delusion throughout my entire life.

●

Moreover, I am very lonesome, and poor, as I have already said,
too healthy, and also too inquisitive. And even when one possesses
so little, at that moment when someone comes tripping in,
all promises, and almost trips over his tongue
in his eagerness…
Incidentally, on closer study the fragments
were not exactly the smallest imaginable,
slightly bigger perhaps than a pea.

Ah! Might these fragments be "foreign bodies"?…
An appalling thought. How come I didn't think of that before?
Already swimming in his wake, I am suddenly startled
by the abruptness of our departure.
On our way I notice that we are out of step with each other —
but only once we are on our way!
Stunned, I sink into the nearest chair, by
the window or the door, what blessings chairs
have been over the years! I sit down again and catch
my breath. Secretly I shake the water from his wake
off my feet. And again I curse

my politeness which, you see, is what continues
to plunge me into misfortune.
But it can't carry on this way!
The moment is approaching when I will be off, in a flash.
Still visibly here in my chair, nothing seems to have changed,
yet looking out of a window
has always given me courage.
It could go on like this for years…
But I swear to you:
in *reality*, in *my* reality that is,
I have silently slipped away.
My body, though, has to carry the can,
because this situation demands superhuman resistance.
Then I develop a stomach ulcer,
a hunchback, or a fever of "unknown origin".
The expedition ends in hospital.
And that is my deliverance, for my illnesses
are my salvation, and my rebirths.

•

After forty-three years, this life
has not become "*my* life." It could just as well
be someone else's life.
Only once this unbearable repetition of events
has come to an end will it become my life…
Which will never happen, not until my death.

What I lost was not worthy of anything except
being lost.
Except for one thing! Except for you, Christian.
I can't understand it! Did that really happen?
It was my fault! My cowardice!

●

Sometimes even the sound of my own breath
embarrasses me. I bless the passing of time.
Rapt in my feelings of adoration since my
blessed childhood marriage in white, I feel that
I am slowly turning white…
Swimming out into the whiteness…
in order to unite at last indissolubly with the white image.
And that is my imploring gesture, but at the same time
"our knife, which is better than a friend".

Written in a state of great anxiety on 24th of February 1959.

●

LES JEUX À DEUX

This text, like the others she writes in Paris and Ermenonville, was produced directly after meeting the white man and accompanied by drawings. Bellmer gives her a music album containing Bellini's opera, Norma; *she draws imaginary portraits of the people who appear in the opera on the sheet-music, and writes her text very carefully on coloured paper which she then glues inside the album.*

Rules of the Games:

1. No more than two people are allowed to play the *Jeux à deux.*
2. The participants consist of A, a male player, and B, a female player.
3. The participants must not have exchanged any sort of tendernesses other than a gaze or a smile before the start of the games.
4. The players are not to come into close physical proximity with one another during the games. The games seem to run smoothest when A sits at the North Pole, and B at the East Pole.
5. The symbolic form of the *Jeux à deux* is the circle, in other words, the game has no beginning or end.
6. The inner states that the two players must develop during the games are:
   Distance
   Concentration
   Meditation
7. Should a *tête-à-tête* occur, it is important that the players should view this misfortune not as an opportunity, but as a mishap. In such cases the more far-sighted of the two must leave at once.
8. If the players fail to observe point 7 of the rules, the *Jeux à deux* are to be discontinued at once.
9. Point 9 of the rules allows those players who have conscientiously obeyed all the previous rules of the *Jeux à deux*, to die together, but only allows the players to accomplish their mutual death between the hours of 9 p.m. and 9 a.m., or between 9 a.m. and 9 p.m.

Prelude to the Jeux à deux

Romantica, 9.9.99 B.C.

1st. Meeting

Norma is taken by Pollion, her husband, to meet Flavius for the first time. Norma enters Flavius's study, shy and withdrawn. The study itself seems dark to her compared to the bright apparition that rises up to her left, and that has nothing human about it apart from a small, cold head which floats just beneath the high ceiling, while three metres below its feet have melted into clouds. Norma looks into the apparition's eyes with effort, then lowers her gaze before the coldness of the inhuman Flavius. Flavius shrinks to the size of a normal man, and extends to Norma his weightless hand. Forewarned, she resolves to avoid his gaze. She waits impassively for the end of the audience, and is relieved when she and Pollion leave together.

2nd. Meeting

The next day. The same scene at the same place and the same time. Once again Flavius looks down at Norma from his inhuman elevation with an evil and searching gaze, only to return quickly to normal human size and extend to her his weightless hand. He offers her an armchair opposite his. Norma does not accept. She hides herself behind him on an uncomfortable chair and immerses herself in Druidic thoughts. Flavius edges his chair round during his audience with Pollion so as to cast Norma a look filled with respect. Norma loses herself in contemplation of Flavius's stooped shoulders. Shortly before the end of this meeting Flavius leaves his chamber with Pollion. Flavius is the first to return. For three seconds Norma remains, her eyes lowered, like a blind stone under Flavius's gaze, which, as she knows, is the forbidden room, the arena in which the *Jeux à deux* are played, and she must never enter, if the circle — formed by Flavius and Norma, and which now contains them — is not to be broken.

Flavius, moved by Norma's readiness to participate with him in the *Jeux à deux*, turns away.

Pollion enters the room and they leave Flavius's house.

3rd. Meeting

Once again Pollion takes Norma to Flavius's house. Flavius's slave-girl takes her to a different chamber. Norma knows in advance that she will not witness Flavius's powers of extension in this room. Indeed, Flavius enters the room right then in his normal size. Norma's fear has left her, she looks at Flavius without embarrassment. At one point she makes him smile. He asks the couple to dine with him, and offers Norma the seat to his right. While serving the exquisite meal, Flavius's slave-girl drops a silver platter, which lands on the floor with a great crash. Norma attaches significance to the incident: the slave-girl seems to have seen someone who has returned from the dead, standing beside her master — a dead person whose aura has not left the house.

Shortly afterwards Norma mentions an insignificant occurrence in Romantica that is also occupying Flavius's thoughts at that same moment. Flavius draws attention to the similarity of their thoughts with a cheerful remark.

After the banquet Flavius calls for drinks and for musicians. The music drives Norma to the brink of madness, of rapturous fear. Flavius observes Norma and receives the first intimacy from her as if it were a secret, for she whispers it to him in the language of the Druids. Norma, a Druid herself, knows that she is listening to the forbidden music of the departed Druids, and this awakens in the lovers a desire for death.

The *Jeux à deux* begin under Norma's raised, hearkening finger.

The prelude has come to its end.

I. *The Game of Incorporation*

As Norma, accompanied by Pollion, distances herself step by step from Flavius, his house and his street, she senses that she is walking step by step towards him. Flavius, left on his own, sits down as if dumbstruck in the armchair in which Norma had raised her finger several minutes earlier, giving the signal to start the first of the *Jeux à deux*. He begins by concentrating on the event. This is called: NORMA HAS APPEARED, and with a cool head Flavius starts to consider its possible consequences. Norma's inaccessibility threatens to destroy his peace of mind for some time to come. Norma must therefore be annihilated by Flavius. Flavius closes his eyes and summons Norma using all his powers of concentration. He gradually solidifies the hazy aspects of her apparition until she stands before him in person. With the aid of his musicians, with the growing power of his mind concentrated on Norma, who at this critical moment is lying in bed at home in the posture of the will-less woman, ready to abandon herself to fear and to death, Flavius succeeds in seizing Norma and is thus able to commence the process of incorporating her.

The actual incorporation of another can only be accomplished by someone in Flavius's situation, by a person burning with the red augury of a woman's seduction, and who counters this red with the white of his purest resistance. Gradually the purple of ice precipitates out from this power-play, forming the climate in which the game of incorporation can flourish.

Norma feels her incorporation by Flavius as like a softening of the marrow, as if the blood in her veins were ebbing away and her senses dissolving. Flavius first releases the softness in Norma: her fear, her confiding nature, her tenderness, her somnolence, her motherliness, her childishness, her playfulness, her sadness, her smiles, her tears and the embrace of her arms. He gulps down all these sweet black draughts with an ever-increasing thirst. At home, Norma enters that most solitary of states: abandonment by her own self, and the drinker remains unaffected by her attempts to protect herself from him. Flavius must intensify his powers against Norma's three- to nine-fold duplications of herself, which are beginning to populate his room, his house. He must leap at her hair, at the sparkle in her eyes, at her mouth in order to tear her down from the ceiling, to pull her out from the folds of the door curtain in which she is hiding. A second Norma crouching beneath the table, a third clasping the main gate, a fourth and a fifth who attempt to rescue themselves by clinging to a candelabrum, or a statue…

Flavius begins to gnash his teeth, his gaze turns murderous. He tears one piece after another down from these whirling, shrouded apparitions, dashes them to pieces and tramples them underfoot, tears at them with his teeth and swallows them. Days and nights pass… Norma turns pale. She spends most of this game of incorporation lying on her bed. She feels dizzy whenever she gets up. Her empty eyes, her hollow cheeks, her emaciated body — she is the picture of someone at death's door. Despite her intelligent willingness to participate in the game of incorporation, she ends up cowering in an attitude of defence and resistance. Her growing feeling of absence awakens an instinct of self-preservation in her, which Flavius can only overpower by redoubling his efforts. In his desperation he believes that there is no end to it — time and again Norma succeeds only partially in appearing to him — her delicate hand waves to him through the window in a sad gesture of greeting. Flavius catches the hand in his teeth, the bones crack, the sweat streams down his face and back. Norma's smile, Norma's foot shyly poised to dance…

Flavius, by now on the verge of tears, destroys her smile, rips apart her foot, and requires seven desolate days and seven nights before he succeeds in incorporating this woman and restoring his peace and dignity. On the seventh day the two of them, Flavius and Norma, were in an unusual but mutually different state. Flavius, still fired by the fever of his work of destruction, suddenly realised[62] that the repast of the last seven days and seven nights had put him in a sanguine mood. He folded his hands together, propped them under his mouth and chin, and concealed a proud and contented smile. He closed his eyes, and meditated on Norma, on a Norma who had turned white, and he sensed that he too turned white when he thought of her, his white cloud. White! White and weightless, they floated towards each other like two clouds.

II. *The Game of Harmony*

This game begins on the evening of the seventh day following the game of incorporation. On this evening Flavius goes to bed early. Norma likewise retires to her chamber at home at the ninth hour. Both of them, one in the north, the other in the east of the city — begin thinking of each other. They recall their voices and gestures, the little they know about each other. Both are still thoroughly exhausted from the exertions of the Game of Incorporation. Their rooms are dark, their windows open, their reveries revolve around the play of moonlight and shadows. Here each discovers the white, cloud-like image of the other, and as Norma closes her tired eyes in order to fall asleep, Flavius beds himself down inside her. The two sleep soundly inside one another, like a sarcophagus inside the other's sarcophagus, and in moments of half-wakefulness they are blissfully aware of their incomparable harmony, which is as great as the harmony mothers sometimes experience with their unborn child. Norma awakes early next morning and as she awakens she becomes aware of Flavius's presence in her outstretched body. They open their eyes together. Norma straightens herself up, followed by Flavius, and they slip out of one another. Flavius "returns" to his own house. The day remains bright and fair under the spell of the previous night, and the days following drift past in calm, fair breaths like the summer wind, until the next game begins.

III. *The Game of Innocuous Reality*

This game proceeds by its own accord, just like chance. It is not at all dangerous, as will be seen, because it is played before witnesses. We will describe three versions here.

1. The day after the Game of Harmony has ended, Flavius, leaning on a column in the Temple of Irminus, happens to see the couple wandering past. He sees from their beautiful clothes that they are on their way to a festival. The grass-wind of harvest time blows through Romantica and raises up Norma's hair like two wings. Her feet are stretched like a bird's beak. She floats over a stone — then she turns to Pollion, and their shoulders and hips brush one another. Flavius cannot watch the dignified couple without a sense of admiration. He cannot but feel moved when he sees their affection for each another, which is based on a sound knowledge of suffering and misfortune and flourishes in that fertile soil. Norma's and Pollion's secret is their shared panic and their disdain for happiness.

Using his ability to extend himself wherever the unexpected prompts his desire to grow, Flavius shoots out at them like a beam of light. They have the impression that he is flying towards them like an arrow. An arrow from a bow of joy. He smiles. A rare event. Flavius has the smile of one who cannot believe his own good fortune, the radiance of enraptured terror, the light of a man smiled on by chance. Norma regards Flavius as if he were an apparition. She watches the years fall from him. For one moment, an icy, heart-rending fire welds the three of them into an ephemeral ring, until they bid one another farewell. The moment their hands touch the enchantment disappears, but afterwards the day floats by in a curious beauty like the clouds above the Temple of Irminus in the depths of the night with no night towards the end of July 99.

2. During a banquet, Norma, who becomes small and quiet in a new, innocuous reality shared with Flavius, wishes to have no mouth, thus reducing the charm radiated by her presence to nothing. Flavius, who has nothing to fear from perceiving, or being beheld by, nothingness, turns his redoubled attention away from the emptiness that has opened on his right, towards the men at the table. From now on the white nothingness on his right is unable even to breathe of his breath. Flavius is content, Norma is content. When the whiteness casts its eyes on whiteness, which occurs later and far from this table, while Flavius is discussing the situation in Romantica, the game is still in progress. The player who manages to get furthest away from the other, while both are together, and before witnesses, wins the game.

3. It is dangerous for the players to linger together in the place of their mutual understanding; a murderous aura will drift towards where the *Jeux à deux* began and the players will be "hunted down relentlessly" by Druid spirits — "that fearful lineage of the night" — who wish "to cast a lasso around their fleeing feet." *This* is the place where the red will incarnadine the whiteness. Here, and here alone!

Norma ascends the steps to Flavius's palace with Pollion, her mind beset by fear. The redness, the hot redness floats into her. She uses her power and wisdom as a Druidess to find a way out. A vision comes to her assistance, an image at once sad and sublime: Norma clearly sees the highest dignitaries of Romantica walking down the steps carrying Flavius in a coffin on their shoulders. The procession passes through her, the redness disappears and she appears as white as a lily before Flavius and his guests. Delighted to meet, they quickly disengage their eyes, which are growing large — and are warned. They have not yet infringed any of the rules of the game, but Flavius must avoid repeating the Game of Incorporation if he does not wish to abandon Norma to a fatal illness and himself to madness. They want to live and continue their games, however: this place must be avoided from now on.

IV. *The Game of Dangerous Unreality*

This game proceeds of its own accord, just like chance. It appears to the players in a dream, and once dreamt it leaves in them the desire to dream beyond all measure. Only unreality can suspend the rule of distance. The players are allowed to meet privately, without witnesses, and to spend hours or whole lifetimes, it seems, with one another. For this reason the more far-sighted of the players must ensure that the actions in their dreams correspond to their innocuous actions in reality, meaning that distance must also be maintained in their dreams, as will presently be seen.

1. After the Game of Innocuous Reality, Flavius and Norma dream their first dream together. Immediately after each has gone to bed in their houses to the north and the east, they meet one another in a flat landscape in dazzling, beautiful weather, in sun and wind, and walk, walk together, aimlessly…

Once again Flavius's years have fallen from him and his bright smile seems to radiate eternal youth. Something indestructible presides over them during this long walk. The state of beatitude described by Eastern poets. A freedom from desire and intention, that which is before all things and is without end. Not a touch, not a word, simply this walking in the light of the glorious day, simply these smiles.

On waking up alone once more, they are astonished — each separately — at the mutual understanding they had experienced during their first walk together, which neither had ever felt before on such an outing, for it is generally believed that the first walk a man and woman take together is very revealing.

2. Several nights later, Flavius is fast asleep when he is brought to half-wakefulness by a dream-invitation from Norma to play once more with her the

Game of Dangerous Unreality. Flavius — who the previous day had chanced to hear Norma's name mentioned several times by friends and strangers when they described the wife of the Proconsul as a unique figure among the women of Romantica — brusquely refuses her. He is aware how dangerous it is to play the unreal games in the climate of the purple of ice. This climate had remained with Flavius all night long. He resorts to a strong sleeping draught so that Norma's calls cannot reach him, and sinks into a stupor. Norma's dream takes place before Flavius's locked door: she is unable to see him. In her dream she is told that Flavius is not granting any audiences today. Nevertheless, the thoughtless woman wanders for one whole night from one door of the palace to the next, down empty corridors and staircases. At one point she thinks she can hear Flavius's voice behind a locked and guarded door, dictating to his scribe. Something resembling an icy warning issues from this door, and Norma awakens, ashamed — and understands.

V. *The Game of Apparent Garrulousness*

It is well known that lovers have a need to conduct endless conversations. This need is granted infinite scope in the *Jeux à deux*. The word "apparent" is used because these conversations should not be conducted *tête-à-tête*, but at a distance, with the players gazing at one another across empty space from far off. Their endless nature prevents any examples of their apparent garrulousness being given here.

VI. *The Game of Apparent Activities*

This game is wordless and may assume various forms. We shall give a few examples.

1. The participants play cat's cradle.

They sit opposite one another, and A begins with a length of string tied into a loop (circle), which he entwines round his fingers following the classical motifs, then invites B to take the string figure, such as this one here: from his fingers. B knows that she must not touch his fingers in the process.

This a game of tenderness, during which B might fall in a faint at A's feet, were it reality. This game is likewise played at a distance from one another.

2. The participants play the Eye Game:

They sit — or so it seems — opposite one another, and A begins by tying a gaze in a loop and wrapping it around his eyes according to classical motifs, before inviting B to remove the gaze from his eyes, to withstand it, and then return it. This is an evil game, during which B could fall dead at A's feet if the actions were *real*.

Fainting fits and incidents of death are a rarity, however, in the Game of Apparent Activities.

VII. *The Game of Emaciation*

The years go by and, tired of the *Jeux à deux*, Flavius and Norma deliver a rapid succession of rude insults to their health. But to anyone who scorns all that is "precious and priceless", she shows her inestimable backside, and whoever sees *that* is filled with the desire to die.

VIII. *The Game of the Final Wish*

In this game the players propagate a wish within their surroundings — until it becomes so compelling that their surroundings fulfil that wish.

Flavius and Norma are unexpectedly made guests of honour at a late night garden party.

Reclining beside one another, their dignity so beguiles the highest dignitaries of Romantica that they are granted their request to be left alone while they die.

IX. *The Final Game*

No one should play this game if they are afraid of death. No one should play this game if they are afraid of life. The desire for death and the joy of living mingle in a terrible way in the eyes of lovers who have no future.

The next day Romantica is in a state of guilt and rage. Dead but unmarked, the two had escaped the consequences of their love. Only reluctantly was it admitted that they had fallen victim to the power of their eyes.

Flavius and Norma were thrown to the dogs to be eaten.

The white man gives her his books (what an adventure for her to read them), and afterwards she returns to writing, after a long interval.

The result is the "Fictitious Letters",[63] an imaginary correspondence between him and her. At this moment in time she is suffering from serious anaemia. A million red corpuscles have deserted her body in a mysterious way, while at the same time her body is covered with countless red spots from an allergy — only her face remains unscathed. A tedious treatment follows, involving various skin specialists and medications for this complaint. She swallows one ampule after another — filled with blood from animal livers — so as to overcome this anaemia which is making her tired and dizzy.

Gradually the red rash disappears, which she refers to somewhat ironically as the "whiteness with the red spot", or the "purple of ice." (His colours! Red and white.) Indeed, she has grown very pale and hopes she will at last come to resemble him.

The imaginary correspondence, written in a careful hand, fills a small book bound in black leather. These letters are too sentimental to be included here. An interesting manuscript comes into being during a bout of jaundice. Under the influence of a mild fever, she writes *The House of Illnesses*, and illustrates it with explanatory drawings. At present the author is too tired to type up this manuscript, which is why it is omitted here.

Once again the author is fed up to the back teeth with life, and now that she has reached her fiftieth year, she hopes to die of insurmountable boredom.

FLAVIUS: the white man
NORMA: herself

Completed on the 22nd of February, 1967

IN AMBUSH

The robber is lying in ambush by the roadside. Waiting. His patience is as tenacious as syrup and sweet as his desire to murder. He chews the wet grass and lies snugly beneath the warm black belly of his faithful horse. His patience is as deep as the sea that Captain Ahab sailed across to kill the white whale, Moby Dick. Both he and Ahab are romantics and lust for fame and glory. Elsewhere the Black Baron is standing behind a long wooden bench waiting for customers. He sells women's heads fashioned in wax, with their faces made up like snakes. The Black Baron curls their locks around his long, grimy fingers.

Their long, waxen necks are adorned with bright strings of glass beads, and flowers grow in and out of their ears. They are pale and noble and are waiting for a new owner. The rogue's sweetheart stands close by, her eyes are tired and she has tears in her lashes. She would love to be one of the white brides who are continuously streaming from the church of Saint-Médard. But she lacks the courage to seize opportunities when they come, and also does not know how to perform the wedding dance. The orange traders have dropped their prices and the next harvest in Batavia is already ruined. Nobody has that way of gently stroking my body that the Black Baron has, with his long, yellow fingers. I walk with him through the rain and watch him. He is deep in my dreams by day and by night, like the grey castle in Spain. I love him like myself, and where you go I will follow. Your land is my land, and where you die I will die too, and there I will be buried.[64] Yet another white bride leaves the church and the photographer fires his flash into the air. It is raining in Rashomon's Forest and the rogue's sweetheart walks slowly and sadly across the street to buy some bitter chocolate.

Meanwhile the woman in the tall white hat and the white veil is approaching slowly through the forest on a white horse. Her spouse holds her tiny, cold hand with reverence and is not afraid of murderers. Four priests and a woodcutter are sitting under the open roof of the temple which rests on four round pillars. The rain does not let up and a mist hangs low amidst the trees. It is an interminably sad and completely white day. The five witnesses give five different accounts of the murder.

Everyone saw it quite clearly and envies the others' descriptions. It is very quiet in the forest when Rashomon awakes from a long, deep sleep. He walks a little way along the old path and not even a twig can be heard cracking under his naked feet. The white woman brushes the white veil from her forehead and looks around. There is not a sound to be heard.

It is a drowsy day. The moss glistens with moisture, it has drunk itself full like a sponge. The hour of death is near and the samurai looks gloomily at the rain. He has to assume responsibility for his wife. She trembles like a white, sweet blancmange in a fine porcelain dish. She does not love her husband and would have left him long ago, had he not been rich, and an aristocrat. She has no children. Her breasts are too precious for her to suckle small animals. They ride and ride, and still no hostelry in sight. The coming night will be dangerous and there will be no pillows on which to lay their heads, nor blankets for cover.

The Black Baron plucks a Queen of Hearts from his wallet with his long fingers, and skilfully makes it vanish in the damp air. A black King of Spades follows close on her heels and politely doffs his crown.

It is time to cook the onion soup and dry the wet locks of the waxen women's heads. The Black Baron loves small slender girls and is on good terms with the vice squad. He draws deeply on a marihuana cigarette, which is as thin as a match, and waits for the clock-tower to strike midday. Days like this are so sombre, and the sun is far away. It makes you so tired you could lie down on the filthy bed. Nothing is ever laundered here, and the patriarch uses his bath only once every three months.

The five witnesses from the forest temple make their way to the Palace of Justice. It looks magnificent with its one hundred large, open windows facing the sun. The judges are strict and impatient and await the head that is to roll. The executioner whets his axe and encrusts its handle with precious stones. No buyers are anywhere to be seen and the clock-tower strikes midday. The Black Baron's pockets are empty. He turns them inside out and a few crumbs of tobacco fall to the ground. Broad-footed pigeons waddle across the square like ducks and old ladies throw them pieces of bread. The rain paralyses both life and loins. What is to become of us, the rogue's sweetheart thinks. The soup is as bitter as gall and the bread is stale. This life is terribly hard. I wish I were dead and floating on the lake like beautiful, mad Ophelia. Water lilies entwine themselves in my long, wet hair and the Black Baron dashes off a quick and passionate painting. The police will come and seal the gallery. Too many suicides since the previous exhibition; young couples who play at Romeo and Juliet. Carefree and loving couples who laugh at their parents' sadness. They carefully prepare their deaths with a shiny gold pocket watch. Burning, igniting of lusting loins with hissing church-oil thunder.[65] Donkey lie down in sugar. Flames lick the nun's tail. Mouth laughing, teeth as white as tiny springtime clouds. Soon it will be warmer. The samurai lets go of his wife's tiny hand. He pricks up his ears like a fox. Something is rustling in Rashomon's Forest. An uncanny, subterranean life is rousing, and no one knows what will happen in the next hour. A great calamity is brewing and the white lady, always ready to shed floods of tears, curls up like an affectionate cat in front of the fire. A duel is being carefully prepared. They will fight breast to breast. One of them will prove himself the stronger.

The forest is as wet as a sponge and the white clouds float through it like silent fish, bellies upwards.

Thunderous igniting of lusting loins with hissing church-oil thunder. I have loved you in vain for so long and you did not come. I called you day and night. How could you forsake me like this? You write poems and poison yourself with nights lacking all trace of sleep. I dare not touch you. You love your solitude like a disease, and women seek sanctuary so as to forget their madness for you. They live a life of grey, in grey, and become fat and sluggish, squatting like black spiders in their dusty webs. I light a candle when darkness comes, so that I can study your flat, white chest. A warm, dark shadow forms where your heart is, and it would be easy to bury a long knife there. Your land is my land, and where you die I will die too, and there I will be buried.

I follow you unto death and will die with you, eye to eye. The legend of the samurai and the laughing robber takes place in Rashomon's Forest, where they lie in ambush. The white lady has dismounted from her horse, and in her long, wet clothes, she waits for a miracle. She dreams of violence and is very scared. Her long hair looses itself and hangs down her back. Rashomon draws his long knife from his tunic and sets out on the hunt like a wary tiger. His teeth shine with long, silent laughter. The woman has lain down in the wet grass and dissolves like a white, sweet blancmange.

Her eyes are narrow and she is as inquisitive as a child. She hates her cautious, deferential husband and wishes for his death. She hates his gentleness and interminable goodness.

The five witnesses walk slowly through the rain and step cautiously over the shiny black slugs. The judges tolerate no lies, but each witness tells a different story: an old legend in Rashomon's Forest, and many centuries have passed since then. The woodcutter carries his axe slung over his right shoulder and ponders on the misery of mankind. The world is a vale of woe, the wind moans and the owls awaken. Nobody wants to be last, and the way to the city is long. What awaits us there? We have seen nothing but the truth, and the murder was cruel and drawn out. Today the Black Baron has decided to eat in a restaurant. The foolish white virgins with their boring black spouses fill him with disgust. I sell small knifes for murder, and sweet melons, and when evening arrives the two balconies bow to each other and the black shades from the holy pond in Iware begin to dance. When the wild geese honk the whole year round I no longer hear them.[66] The Black Baron stabs his fork into the greasy mutton and his stomach turns… His stomach wheezes, it's as weak as a pregnant lark. He does not stop smoking even when he eats and behind his chair stands a tall, thin cop. He confiscates the contents of the

Black Baron's pockets, who starts drinking calvados in despair.

A doctor at the neighbouring table rises and threatens him, "If you don't stop you will shortly die."

"I have never enjoyed being alive," the Black Baron says over his shoulder, "I was a melancholy child and never liked marbles. I have eaten too much sugar and my teeth are rotten. My youth was an embalmed mummy-chair and misfortune gnawed away my leg."[67] Your speech is Yes, yes, no, no. Everything beyond that is bad news. The woman in the white veil lies quietly in Rashomon's Forest. She is waiting to embrace the victor. She will spend her twilight years in a teahouse in Tokyo, and no one is there waiting for her. She has become so despicable. Rashomon positions the long knife as deftly as a surgeon. Meanwhile, the Black Baron is illustrating the story of Jack the Ripper. Rashomon slits open the samurai's belly. He wriggles like an earthworm. The forest rings with the woman's wild weeping. She strokes the creases out of her spouse's splendid coat and begins her long, heart-rending lament. A small bird is perched high on a tree and begins to whistle scornfully. Its black, pearly eyes follow the route the five witnesses take along the path deep below. All the windows in the large Palace of Justice are wide open and the sun warms the solemn rooms.

Great stacks of files and documents have been placed at the ready, and a price is put on Rashomon's head.

Rashomon raises his foot and kicks the woman in the face. He has become totally indifferent to everything. He is as hoarse as a crow. Mr. Demon Leg[68] trots through the forest at a faster pace and the owl makes a hole in its nest. The wind blows through the temple on its four round pillars, like those in the arcades in Metz with their stout pigs' feet. It is draughty inside, like a railway station. The summer is still very far off and the days darken early in the afternoon. Everything is sad and quiet and lacks the warmth of a fire. The wood is wet and the fire won't burn. No one far and wide who can tell a good long yarn. How is one to pass the time on a day like this? The waiter stuffs the money into his waistcoat pocket and lays a fresh cloth on the table. The Black Baron reaches the door, he feels heavy and stuffed full of food. He would like to sleep but his eyes refuse to close. He returns to his filthy hotel room and lies down on the bed. The petrol stove emits a lukewarm heat, brown drops of water trickle down the walls. Someone is washing pots and pans in the courtyard. These are familiar sounds, the same every day. The smoke from the chimney pots hangs thick and yellow over the small, dirty courtyard. No joy in living, far and wide. What will come of it? We have lost every scrap of courage. This winter is endless, like a monotonous tune.

I search for you on every path and how I would love to meet you and remain with you for ever. But you avoid me. There is no woman you love and nor have you any friends.

You nurture your solitude like an incurable illness. The man with the hoarse voice sits in the concentration camp and builds the Hotel de L'Esperance, 88 rue Mouffetard, out of matchsticks. We have all grown sick from yearning and I no longer know the way home. Moby Dick swims calmly and nobly through the cold waters of the ocean and waits to take his revenge on Captain Ahab. The captain has carved himself an artificial leg from a whale's tooth and strapped it to his hips. The leather straps creak beneath his jacket. He has turned up his collar and stands on the bridge in the wind. He has an extra ration of rum handed out to the crew. But the men are tired from the long watches. They sleep in their cold bunks and dream of home. The Black Baron lies stretched out on his filthy bed. He dreams of the pictures he wants to paint. He is a slow and painstaking artist and despises the colours. He has a bitter taste in his mouth and his lips are parched. Rashomon pulls apart the tiny fingers that are wrapped around his neck and frees himself once and for all. He mounts his horse and leaves the wailing bundle lying by the roadside.

The Black Baron and Rashomon have never got to know each other. This is because they lived in different times and in different lands. Much more will come to be told about the two of them. They live with the courage of despair. Both of them fall easily in love with very young girls who are still half-children, and maintain their superiority.

Both of them would love to sleep with their daughters. The mothers are not up to much and have been quickly forgotten.

They have grown fat and sluggish, like women in a sanatorium.

The five dissimilar witnesses have reached the town and make their way to the Palace of Justice. The judges have wise, stony faces and wait for the hour of judgement. Rashomon makes his entry into town. He drinks like a fish at an inn and eats a white rabbit. He feels strong and young as never before. He is replete, and feels warm. The cobbles on the street glisten in the rain. Sedan chairs containing the city's gentry sway along the streets and the servants pull their round straw hats down over their foreheads. The gallows is slowly raised and the executioner feels insulted and places his axe back in its case. Which is more degrading? Decapitation or hanging? The judges have decided on the gallows. The rogue's sweetheart still has not returned home. She is hungry. But what is there for her at home? Blows and hunger, tears and a long night without warmth. It is as cold in the arms of the Black Baron as in the arms of death. Everything has become so futile and our ways have nothing in common.

The wax women's heads have been left in the rain on the long bench in the Place St. Médard and the wind caresses their long black locks.

The clock-tower strikes 3 o'clock in the afternoon.

Laughing, Rashomon leaves the inn, crosses the large courtyard and makes his way into the Palace of Justice. His black hair hangs over his forehead in wet curls. His shirt is open at the chest and his heart beats firm and calm. He is sick to death of life. He has taken leave of his senses, and is alone like the ghost in the grey tower. He is sleepless at night and out and about; he forces his way into the town with the pride of a freed animal and now impatiently awaits his final hour. The noose on the gallows sways in the wind, and the windows fill with inquisitive faces. He enters and lies down on the wooden floor, tightly wrapped in his overcoat. Everything is ready. "I saw," the first witness begins, "how Rashomon wound the entrails out of the samurai's belly, like a hurdy-gurdy. I can still hear the screams resounding in my ears. The birds fell silent in the trees and the forest covered its face. Blossoms fall like snow, a sheet of mist envelops the lake and hordes of dark dreams dance their round. My heart is heavy." The judges nod and take notes. The second witness recounts how Rashomon sprang at the white lady from his ambush and took her by force. The samurai had taken flight. No one has seen him since.

The woman waits in Rashomon's cave for his return and gathers herbs to heal his wounds. The third witness saw Rashomon bind the knight to the woman's white body with cords, in order to slay the two of them together with his sword on the forest floor.

The statements of the remaining witnesses were no longer written down. The judges retired to confer and, before night descended, Rashomon was hanged. Head thrown back, lying half-prostrate, his laughter was heard by the whole town, and there was more than one woman who admired him and who would happily have left her husband for his sake. Captain Ahab takes the Indian harpoonist with him in his boat in order to begin the final hunt for the white whale. He is filled with rage and his patience is at an end. The harpoonist buries his weapon in the whale's white back, which is covered with scars from previous frays. The whale lifts the little boat out of the sea and causes it to crash violently back into the depths. Captain Ahab grabs the harpoon from the harpoonist's hand and readies himself to deliver the death blow to Moby Dick. The boat capsizes and they both drown. The ship returns to harbour without its captain. I, who witnessed all this happen, can no longer find peace of mind. Ahab has hunted across all the oceans and is, like the Flying Dutchman, still restlessly under way. Like Moby Dick he is immortal. Neither can be saved. Seafarers never tire of telling the story on winter nights.

The rogue's sweetheart collects the wax heads in a bag, and bloody feet fall left and right onto the street. She trudges up the stairs with her bag to room 42. Their fine noses are grazed and their nostrils flare painfully. The glass dolls' eyes roll out of their sockets and the silken lashes close with weariness. The woman in the white veil has moved to Tokyo. She celebrates her widowhood and opens a brothel. She smokes opium and business prospers. The red light burns day and night above the door. She has become fat and sadistic. The best customers are priests and policemen. The priests pray for the young girls and fill the censer. The beds are soft and covered with white sheets. All day long there is music and sweet pastries. The girls sing with deep voices and miaou like cats. Rashomon is as immortal as Moby Dick and wanders as a spirit in the forest. Snow has fallen in the middle of June.

The temple has long since gone to rack and ruin. Wild red flowers wind about its pillars.

Far, far away in Poland, on the bank of the Dnieper, a little girl sits and weeps. Her clothes are made of calico, sadly she has lost her parents. Far, far away in Poland, on the banks of the Dnieper, that's my home. Captain Ahab passes by and throws a giant jellyfish onto her lap. With tiny, impatient fingers she divides the jellyfish into lots of tiny jellyfish. As night descends she casts them into the sea, where they reunite once more into a giant jellyfish. It swims off out into the deep ocean.

There Ahab is living on a rotten shipwreck. He has taken a seal for his wife. The seal bears him a host of small, lovely white whales. Ahab harbours a bottomless hatred for his children. Floating beneath the sea is a glass organ on which the wind plays like the trumpets of Jericho. The fish swim up on every side and stare in through the church windows. The dead preacher swings the cross carved out of whale bones and sings loudly, praising Jonah in the belly of the whale.

Rashomon lies in his cave with his eyes open wide. The wound on his throat heals. Misfortune is seated beside his bed and rests. The small girl from Poland receives a present of a balloon. She lets go of the string and the balloon flies off to Siberia, where the tea harvest has just commenced. The balloon flies on further and attaches itself to the foot of a white dove. They couple and produce strange children made of rubber and feathers. An old Gregorian chant, sung by 200 boys, brings tears to my eyes. Rashomon lies in his cave with his eyes open and wraps his long hair round his neck. In his hotel room the Black Baron splays his legs and assumes an indecent pose. The vice squad sets to work, sealing the door with pitch and sulphur. The rogue's sweetheart squats in a corner of the corridor and places her ear to the wall. She hears all the bleak water streaming and gurgling in the wall. The water flows out of the holes in the walls and down the stairs. Quiet wind, the whale-egg flows, cloud-silk beckons.[69] A crate wants to wash ashore and all the bleak waters in the wall cease to flow. The rogue's sweetheart waits in her corner for evening to arrive. I look at you and you close your eyes and I lull you to sleep. I rock you like my little child and kiss your temples and forehead and cheeks.

You laugh in your sleep, and the next day you are as if new-born. I dance on my claws along your back and the black curtain is rent asunder. Torrents rush into Rashomon's Forest and black mud rises up into the branches.

Moss has grown over the samurai and his name is damned for all eternity. Rashomon waits for the rain to end. He rubs his burning eyes and builds a trap, strong enough to hold a lion. He catches a deer in it and plays with it as if with a kitten. He roasts it and devours it and belches and falls asleep again. Now he is alone for the fourth time. No prospect of a companion. A scribe from China comes wandering past and stays with Rashomon while autumn sets in. Rashomon becomes as polished as ivory and his speech becomes gracious. Nevertheless he has the desire to set out on another raid. He sends the scholar away without having learned how to write. The beautiful, serious forest has long since turned green. Nightingales sing the whole night long. A new crime demands to be prepared. He wraps himself in his cloak and lies down beneath the trees close to the path. A young girl comes walking by in her Sunday clothes. She is swaying her hips and singing. Rashomon leaps onto her back like a tiger and buries her beneath himself.

He undergoes a lengthy passion and his legs become damp. He strangles her and dismembers her with his knife. He plants her head with its long sweet hair on a bamboo cane, and the ravens come and peck out her eyes.

Rashomon lies down in the lion pit and waits for the tiger. The tiger appears and is captured.

Rashomon takes it into his cave as his companion and they live together.

They are both wild and independent and get on well. The rogue's sweetheart has forced her way through the door sealed with pitch and sulphur and lies down quietly beside the Black Baron. A lantern burns in the courtyard and a tap runs the whole night long. They make love and remain lying entwined. Why don't you come when I call. I stick long pins into your photograph and wish you the worst. You love neither a man nor a woman and nurture your solitude like an illness. I need you badly but am too proud to visit you. Better that I dream of you as if you did not even exist. Wherever you go, I shall not go. I detest your land and despise your people. I shall be glad when you die and an owl screams the whole night long at your burial place. Spiders scamper out of the ivy and run back and forth over your grave and no one can read the inscription on your tombstone.

The Black Baron stirs quietly in his sleep and talks as he dreams. Tomorrow I shall paint an indecent picture with open trousers and lots of feet and hands occupying themselves in dubious ways. Your speech is black and white and yes, yes and no, no. Two brave men together is no improvement, which is why the tiger soon left Rashomon. Captain Ahab swims around the Cape of Good Hope with his wife, and they let themselves drift with the current. The seal's eyes are a warm, dark brown and her throat is covered with bite marks. She must give birth incessantly to little white whales. That is Moby Dick's curse.

And as you make your bed, so you must lie on it, there is no one to tuck you in. And when someone walks, it will be me, and when someone falls, it will be you. Captain Ahab remains Moby Dick's sworn enemy and hunts him tirelessly into the realm of the shades. He can never forgive him the loss of his leg and he suffers greatly under the burden of the polished whale tooth. In a rage he stabs the tooth deep into the seal's body. The whale tooth is as sensitive as the nerve in a tooth.

After they have got up they tap on the wall of the room from top to bottom to find the treasure. They remove a stone from the wall and find a dried embryo which looks like an appendix preserved in alcohol. Long ago this house had been a convent and a nun had given birth on her own. On this morning the Black Baron takes on his own shoulders the sale of the heads and his sweetheart remains in bed. She makes fresh coffee for herself and slurps it down, hot and sweet. She washes the Baron's seed from her long legs and sweeps the room. She washes the floor, the dishes, and the filth-encrusted windows. Then she crawls back into bed and begins her childish litany once more: Wherever you go I shall leave, for your land is a pauper's kitchen. I shall plant no flowers where you die and scatter sharp stones on your grave. Your name is already forgotten and no one remembers you. A dog passes by, raises its leg, and kicks up the dirt.

I no longer wait for you and I no longer dream of you. I laugh in your face and roll myself up into a ball. I have become unassailable.

The lovely armchair opposite me is empty. The lamp has been extinguished and

I have torn all your letters and pictures into pieces. You have taken your clothes from my wardrobe and your scent has disappeared with them. You have gone on a long voyage and sail the seas in a ship. The hoarse sound of your voice is still in my ears. I am sad without you, but there is nothing to be done about it. The hunched-backed flower-seller on the windy street corner claps both hands to his face and weeps. And now his lame wife has presented him with a baby but he continues crying, uncontrollably. The garlic vendor with the wooden leg plays French waltzes on his mouth organ and the little children dance along behind him. They are crazy about the long, uncanny stories he tells them on the street corners. I can still feel the curved palms of your hands and the soft pressure of your fingers. One has to be brave and stand alone, that is a noble stance. I embrace you for the last time and soon we shall have forgotten everything, just as we will be forgotten.

The Black Baron pulls his handkerchief from his trouser pocket, and a pale wax woman's hand falls from it. A cop jumps at it, nose first, and examines the hand with a magnifying glass, looking for traces of blood. Embarrassed, the circle of spectators stare at the ground. At last the Black Baron sells a wax woman's head to a hairdresser. He celebrates with a glass of red wine at the tobacconist's. His trousers start to slip. He has grown skinny and feels feverish.

A one-time hussar is standing on a watchtower in Africa, scanning the plain through a telescope. It is just before sunrise. A row of large bushes edges slowly across the plain up to the palisade gateway of the Okahandja fortress. The hussar, who is now a cavalry major, realises what is going on. The Hereros have dug up bushes and tied them to their bodies. They are about to storm the fortress. English traders have sold them rifles. During the previous nights the Hereros had sacked farmsteads and murdered their owners. It was the start of the insurrection.

The Hereros call the cavalry major Omuhona Omunene, which means great chief. Samuel Herero is the king. He is blind and has many wives with withered breasts. His head is adorned with white shells. He has six strong sons with large huts. The day of his death will be commemorated and a grave will be built for him with large stones. The trees about it will be hung with antlers. The king was not pleased by the white man with the glass eye. Pluck out your other eye as well. The white man could not do it and the king turned his back on him in contempt.

Polly's father has arrived in Paris. He is searching for his stepson, Mack the Knife. He has rented rooms in a brothel on the Place Pigalle and lets himself be entertained by the whores. They bring him food and drink and he forgets Polly, his wife, who is back in Berlin expecting a child.

And as you make your bed so you must lie on it. But no one will tuck you in. And when someone walks, it will be me. And when someone falls, it will be you. This morning the Black Baron's thing was smouldering in the cold room. That's how warm it felt in the belly of the rogue's sweetheart.

Introduction

1. All quotes not otherwise identified are from *The Man of Jasmine*, in Unica Zürn, *Gesamtausgabe*, vol. 4.1., Berlin, 1991, pp.135-255

2. *Dunkler Frühling*, Hamburg, 1969, p.9, published in English as *Dark Spring*.

3. *Crécy Notebook*, 1970, in: Zürn, *Gesamtausgabe*, vol. 5, *Aufzeichnungen*, Berlin, 1989.

4. Page 26 in this edition.

5. *Die Begegnung mit Hans Bellmer*, 1970, in Zürn, *Gesamtausgabe*, vol. 5, Berlin, 1989, p.109

6. *Crécy Notebook*, Zürn, *Gesamtausgabe*, vol. 5, p.7.

7. *L'Anatomie de l'image*, Paris, 1957; the essay on anagrams appeared as an afterword to Zürn's publication *Hexentexte*, Berlin, 1954.

8. Notizen einer Blutarmen, Zürn, *Gesamtausgabe* vol. 4. 1. p. 29

9. Page 29 in this edition.

10. These include Dr. Jean-François Rabain in his essay *"Zu Unica Zürn: 'Der Mann im Jasmin'"*, in *Der Mann im Jasmin*, Berlin 1977, pp.188-195, and the recent editors of her works in Germany: Inge Morgenroth (*Das Weiße mit dem roten Punkt*, Berlin, 1981) and Sabine Scholl (Unica Zürn, *Fehler Fallen Kunst*, Frankfurt am Main, 1990, and *Freibord* 65, Vienna, 1988). Dr. Rabain focuses on Zürn's mother as the source of Zürn's later problems (the phallic, engulfing mother who, in an oedipal clinch, forbids her encounters with men), while the female interpreters find more mileage in her father. The figure in *The Man of Jasmine* of the "beautiful, dangerous creature: a girl and a snake in one — with long tresses, a girl and a snake in one," varies between Rabain and Morgenroth, for instance, as an image of the smothering mother mentioned above, and that of a woman upon whom "a careful operation is performed upon it so as to remove anything [she] might use to wreak this destruction."

11. *Dark Spring* notably contains passages that reveal the intensity of her childhood preoccupation with her father and with other heroic fantasy figures who prefigure the four kings in *The Man of Jasmine* — powerful exotic beings who inspire her with fear and admiration, and who ravish and kill her in her nocturnal imaginings. The mortal enemy in *The House of Illnesses* also has his counterpart in the form of her (presumably real) brother, who likewise rapes her and threatens her with death if she tells her mother what he has done.

12. In *Fehler Fallen Kunst*, Sabine Scholl is incensed by Bellmer's photographic action with

Unica Zürn, in which he parcelled up her naked body with string to create a new landscape, new breasts and new organs (the cover illustration of *Le Surréalisme, même* 4, 1958, consisted of one of these photographs). Scholl notes that Zürn never referred to these photographs, but fails to mention in this context the passages in *Dark Spring* in which the young girl is described as experiencing sensual enjoyment from being brutally bound and mishandled during games of cowboys and Indians.

13. *Les Jeux de la poupée*, written in 1937 and published in Paris, 1949.

14. Bellmer, "*Nachwort*", in Zürn, *Hexentexte*, Galerie Spranger, Berlin, 1954.

15. *Notes on Her Last (?) Crisis*, pp.111-134.

16. "The Anatomy of Love", in *The Doll*, Atlas Press, p.133.

17. In two passages in *Dark Spring*, the young girl yearns for a male complement to fill the emptiness that follows masturbation.

18. As pointed out by Sabine Scholl, *Freibord, op. cit.*

19. The images of male and female interlocked with one another appear in several of Zürn's texts. The two lovers in *Les Jeux à Deux* rest in one another as if in a sarcophagus. See the citation from *Notes of an Anaemic*, that begins "Someone is travelling inside me…", in the main text here p.22, and in *The House of Illnesses* she explores the interior of what appears to be her own body, while kept in control by a male-dominated institution.

20. "The Whiteness with the Red Spot", p.142.

21. *The Man of Jasmine*, P.151.

The Man of Jasmine

22. A 1960s comedy crime film, starring Jack Hawkins.

23. The friend is obviously Hans Bellmer.

24. *Euer Tag heisst: hart / Eure Augen: sein. / Eure Haut ist Gesang — euer Rat: seh' ein. / Euer Haus is getarnt. Eure Siege nah. / Eure Tat: ein sarg-geeintes Ruhehaus.*

25. *Nun sucht dich sein sinnendes Auge als Ziel. Kurz / sind unsere Tage und sinken zu schnell zu Eis. — Ach!*

26. *Nach drei Wegen im Regen bilde / im Erwachen Dein Gegen-Bild: Er — / der Magier! — Engel weben Dich in / den Drachenleib. — Ringe im Wege — / lange, beim Regen, werd ich Dein.*

27. *Hinter dieser reinen Stirne / redet ein Herr, reist ein Sinn, / irrt ein Stern in seine Herde, / rennt ein seid'ner Stier. Hier / der Reiter Hintersinn, seine / Nester hinter Indien — Irr-See / Irr-Sinn, heiter sein — Ente der / drei Tinten-Herr — reisen sie / — ein Hindernis! — Retter seiner / Dinten-Herrn — ist es eine Irre?*

28. "And shave off your little rosy beard" is the title of a poem by Hans Arp, which Zürn used for several of her anagram poems.

29. *Tristan neben Isolde. Herber Rauch / irrt ueber das harte Leben. In schon / bleiche Birne aus sternroter Hand / bau'n die Lerchen ihr Nest. Aber rot — / rebenrot schneit es Baldrian-Ruhe.*

30. "*Ernst*" is the German word for "earnest".

31. *Wo regnet's zwischen neun und drei? Es / regnet zwischen uns so neu. Der Winde / Neun ist zur Sechs geworden. Wenn die / Wege rot, renn' zu uns dich weiss. Enden / werden wir, zu siegen! Stunden, schoen / zu erroeten. Schweigend, wissend nun.*

32. *Steig aus der Flasche! Der / siegt, der aus der Flasche / als die Feder gruesst. Ach — / See-Adler, Frische, Du Tag!*

Der Geist aus der Flasche / fragt Dich aus. Der es lese, / schaurig der Edle, fasste / Dich Graus. Fels der Aeste / sag, es rauscht. Die Felder, / als sich das Feuer regte, / lag Erde, Frische des Tau's.

Durst als Gefieder, Asche / aus Glas, fischte der Erde / Gift. Rasch'le, rede aus des / Fasses guter Lach', die der / Drude Leiche frass, sagte / der Geist aus der Flasche.

Sag es aus der Feder Licht, / Tage der Schauder fliesse / Lese das Gesicht der Frau. / Aus der Flasche steig der / Tau. Ed'le Grasfrische des / Flusses, ach, der Tage drei.

Es rauscht das Gefieder, / der Schlaf ist aus. Gerede / der Flasche steig aus der / Figur. Rede sachte als des / Geistes Rauch, da der Fels / des Auges Adel erfrischt.

Ich gruesse das Alte: Feder, / Falter, Scheide des Grau's. / Sag es der Frau: Lichte des / Teufels, dass sich der Arge — / der Geist aus der Flasche — / die Fresse drausgelacht.

33. "*On peut s'amuser tout seul!*": One can have fun on one's own!

34. *Wenn ueber's Jahr der Jasmin blueht, / blueht ueber's Jahr der Jasmin. Wenn / nun der Herbst um's Jahr, liebe wen, ja! / Sah nun Winter um's Jahr, jeder beleb' / sein jahr, jedes wunderbare Blut H M. / Jubel banne des jahres Wut im Herrn, / der ueber's Jahr H M ist. Jub'le an, wenn / er blueht. Ja, Bruder, ha, H M. Wenn sein / Eis und Blut weh' es brenn'. Ja, ja, Herr M. / Wenn ueber's Jahr der Jasmin blueht, / blueht ueber's Jahr der Jasmin. Wenn / Du lebst, ueber's Jahr, ja, H M. Wenn er in / den Nebel irrt, um's Jahr — weh', Busen, ja. / Neuen jahr' wesen, Bruder H*

M, ja. Liebst / Du Messer in Blut? Ja, H. Renne, Jahr web / unsre Lebenswert-Uhr. Ja, H M, ja. Binde / uns sterbend in Ruh'. Leb, H M, ja. Wer / muss neun Jahr' warten? Jeder. Bleib H.

35. Ernst Kreuder's *Die Gesellschaft vom Dachboden* (*The Attic Pretenders*), was the first "best-seller" in Germany after the war, and was one of Zürn's favourite books. The characters in the novel counter the enforced seriousness of life with an anarchic, childlike playfulness.

36. The telephone number 999 relates purely to Zürn's fascination with the number 9, and has no connection with the emergency services, as it does in the UK.

37. "*Quelle vie!*": What a life!

38. "Liberation from hope is complete liberation."

39. *Plume* is a book by Henri Michaux.

40. P.M.U. *Pari mutuel urbain*, a nationwide betting agents for horse racing.

41. H.L.M. Habitation à loyer modéré or municipal housing.

42. *Meeting with Mr. M (My Death).*

43. *Deine Wege ins Hinterland B. / da regnet es blind herein — We — / Weh' — Deliria sind gebete. N — N — N — / Der Wind blaest. Eingehen in / Wahnsinnige Bilder endet in / Leid. Eng is der Wahn. Eben / steigen, dann leiden. Hib! Wer? / Er! Wann? Nie! Eingebildet! / Was? Rien! H — D — S — / Elend beginnt. Dehi — / Dehi — bewegtes Deleria. N — N — N — / Endet das nie? / Nein! G — B — L — I — H — Wer? —*

44. *Nehrus Tod aendert alles — / — Du sanftes Land — / — Sonne und ruhende Fernen — / — uralte Hoelzer — / — zarte, lautlose Frauen — / O altes Zauberland Tod.*

45. "The strange adventures of Mr. K.": The title may have been taken from a painting by Victor Brauner *The Strange Case of Mr. K*, or perhaps a poem by Hans Arp.

46. *Es is kalt. Raben reden um den See. Reh / und Amsel trinken Tee. Rabe, Seher des / Unheils am Abend. Erste Sterne. Rede, K! / Die erste Unke starb sehr elend am / Hik. Nebenan redete der Esel's-Traum. Es / blutete die Nase des armen Herrn K. See, / dunkler See der Raben. Atmen heisst / Leben, heisst rankendes Traeumen der / seltsamen Abenteuer. Die, des herrn K.?*

47. *Die Jugend singt: nun ist das Meer Dein Hafen — ist / Traum und Jagd, des Geistes Innen-Feste, die ihn in / finst're, steinige Tage senden, ja, Du. Und ihm sind / Hand und Sinn mit Ernst gefeit. Ja, Du! — Siege sind / gefundenes Ahnen. Du reist in die Stadt Jim-Sing. / Geh in die juengste Strasse und find AMIN den TI. / Er sagt: ja-nein-einst-nie-Feind-Mut es sind ... Du-DHG. / Geheimsignatur? Jadestein? Du findest den Sinn.*

48. Meaning "the bottom", or "the depths".

49. "*Je suis fou du joie!*": I am crazily happy!

50. "*C'etait un fou*": That was a madman.

51. "*C'est le diablé*": It's the Devil.

52. "*Ah, c'est penible, penible*": Ah, it's so painful, .so painful.

53. "*Quelle bordel, la vie!*": Life's just a brothel!

54. "*On est fou*": I am mad.

Notes on Her Final (?) Crisis

55. Unica Zürn's son.

56. The text has "his", although Christian was not Michaux's son.

57. "*Madame, s'il vous plaît, — à boire s'il vous plaît!*": Madam please — bring me a drink!

58. Franz Werfel (1890-1945): former expressionist poet, writer and playwright, his utopian novel *The Star of the Unborn* was written in Sweden shortly before his death and published (in German and English editions) in 1946.

59. "*C'est ta faute.*": It's your fault.

60. The state owned film monopoly, founded in 1917, which was transformed into a Nazi propaganda machine under Goebbels.

The Whiteness with the Red Spot

61. On 27 December 1957, Zürn wrote in her *Notizen einer Blutarmen* (*Notes of an Anaemic*) about the faces of those close to her, with whom she had identified and who had constituted her life: "The sum of all the faces with whom I have lived has manifested itself. This face exists! At last I have seen it and grasped it in its entirety." in Zürn, *Gesamtausgabe* 4.1, 1991, p.30.

Les Jeux à deux

62.The text for this "game" moves into the past tense at this point.

63. An imaginary correspondence between Zürn and Michaux written in 1957, first published under the title "*Erdachte Briefe*" in Zürn, *Das Weiße mit dem Punkt*, Berlin, 1988.

In Ambush

64. "Your land is my land…" A paraphrase of Ruth 1.17.

65. "Burning, igniting the lusts of loins…": this sentence and the following variation are derived from the first two lines of Zürn's anagram poem *"Toennendes Erz und klingende Schelle"* ("Sonorous Ore and Tinkling Bell"), from 1954.

66. Zürn captures here the tones of the "Farewell Poem" written by Prince Otsu (Japan, 663-686), pretender to the imperial throne, shortly before committing suicide after being falsely accused of plotting rebellion by Empress Jito.

67. Here Zürn paraphrases the lines of her anagram poem *"Meine Jugend ist das Unglueck meines Lebens"* from 1957. The portmanteau *"Mumiensessel"*, "mummy-chair", is a neologism.

68. According to Inge Morgenroth, (*cf.* note 10) the curious German word *"Unholbein"* is applied at one point to describe Captain Ahab in the German translation of Melville's *Moby Dick*. See "Unica Zürn" in Zürn, *Das Weisse mit dem roten Punkt*, Berlin, 1981, p.228, note 103. The word also appears in her anagram poem *Und scheert ihr Rosenbaertlein ab.*

69. From the anagram poem *"Es war ein Kind, das wollte nie"* (1955).

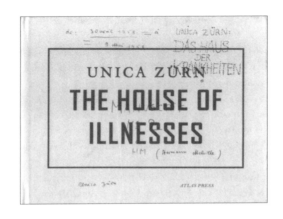

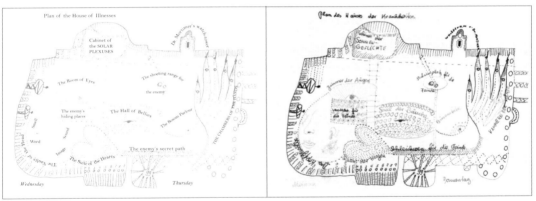

We are offering readers *The House of Illnesses* at the special price of £10 plus postage (UK £2.00, Europe £4.50, everywhere else £6.50). This edition is a complete colour facsimile of Zürn's notebook with the text in a newly revised translation by Malcolm Green. The illustrations are each reproduced with an English key, as shown above. 96pp. hardback, 170 x 215 mm. Please quote the codeword "Jasmine" and order, with your address, from editor@atlaspress.co.uk.

For information on other Atlas Press titles see our website: www.atlaspress.co.uk

For a complete listing of all titles available from Atlas Press
and the London Institute of 'Pataphysics see our online catalogue at:
www.atlaspress.co.uk
To receive automatic notification of new publications
sign up to the emailing list at this website.
Atlas Press, 27 Old Gloucester St., London WC1N 3XX
Trade distribution UK: www.turnaround-uk.com; USA: www.artbook.com

ICH SUCHTE DEN 3 ELTSAMSTEN SATZ

DIE SC

DIE SELTBAMEN ABETEUERN

DES HERRN K

ES IST KALT

DIE SELTSAMEN ABENTEUER DES HERRNK

ES IST KALT RABEN REDEN VON DEN SEE RCH

EIN NEUE DE HR

EHR

DIE SELTSAMEN ABENTEUER DES HERRNK

DIE SELTSAMEN ADENFEYER DES HERRN H

IM AMSEL TRINKEN TEE ABER DES SEHER

ET SEAD GE EE SHRN

SEHR